The Case of the Pisces Moon Murk

Rhiannon D. Elton

The Case of the Pisces Moon Murk © Rhiannon D. Elton 2022
The Wolflock Cases: Book 7
Second edition

ISBN: 978-0-6487636-6-6 (paperback)

First Edition published June 2017
Second Edition published March 2022

info@rhiannoneltonauthor.com

Cover compiled by Rhiannon D. Elton

This is a work of fiction. Names, characters, places, and incidents either are the products of the author's imagination or are used fictitiously. Any resemblance to actual persons, living or dead, businesses, companies, events, or locales is entirely coincidental.

Cataloguing-in-Publication information for this title is listed with the National Library of Australia.

Published in Australia by Rhiannon D. Elton and Pelaia Adventures

This project is supported by the Regional Arts Development Fund (RADF). RADF is a partnership between the Queensland Government and Logan City Council to support arts and culture in regional Queensland.

Dedicated to Cassie,
Your friendship and your strength is ever inspiring to me. Here's to many more laughs, queen of badassery!

Get More of the Magic & Mystery...

subscribe.rhiannoneltonauthor.com/more

If you want more clues, more magic and more mystery, let me know by going to the Wolflock Cases subscribe page.

You'll get clues, maps, sketches, behind the scenes stories, lore and much more! You'll also be the first to know when a new story is coming out so you can solve the mystery before your friends.

If you sign up with the magical link below, you'll also get a free downloadable map to follow Wolflock's journey to Mystentine University.

subscribe.rhiannoneltonauthor.com/more

Declaration of Intention

Merry meet,

The purpose of the books the author writes is to give representation to as many peoples, creatures and landscapes as they can. Although written from the perspective of a Caucasian teenage boy, the author hopes to offer a light into the harmony of different cultures and creeds of people. The author's aim is to promote harmony, understanding and compassion in all areas, while also inspiring readers to stand up against injustice and be critical thinkers in life.

While the author does their best to research, interview and highlight the best parts of people, they are only human and can make mistakes. The author asks you gently educate them by sending them an email in order to discuss anything that may have caused harm to a group of people unintentionally.

The author believes that the cure for ignorance is education, but please approach the topic cordially in order to avoid any knee-jerk cognitive dissonance.

Finally, the viewpoints displayed in the books comes from a particular character and is not necessarily that of the author's. The author seeks to display flaws, growth and human nature on many levels, and hopes that you will analyse the character of the protagonist without adopting any negative behaviours from them.

Merry part, and merry meet again.

CHAPTER 1

Part of the Crew

It was the worst torture he'd ever endured.

"Eye in the boat, Mr Felen! Bear a hand!"

Wolflock set his jaw as he translated the command in his mind.

Pay attention. Help out. But where?

The blisters on his hands stung.

"Unfurl the main sail and keep taut the line!"

Open the mainsail and hang on for dear life.

His arms felt like they were going to shatter.

"Smartly now, lad!"

Hurry up.

The skin on his face felt crunchy from sunburn.

"Square the sail!"

Bring the sail around using both braces and sheets until the yard is athwartship. Who'd have thought such a cold sun could still make my skin this raw...

His back felt as if he was carrying an iron jacket.

"Strike the pennant line!"

Let go of the pennant line, lower the pennant, unhitch the pennant, and make the pennant line.

Even his very bones seemed to ache.

"Belay that, Mr Felen! Geagle's got it!"

Ignore that command.

He made the mistake of letting his shoulders relax as he drew a breath. Captain Blutro rounded on him the moment he slowed.

"Loose the halyard!"

Wolflock ran to the position and untied the rope.

Let it run free.

Blutro's voice was not nearly as pleasant as it had been when he first boarded.

"Alright, Mr Felen! Tie the knot right this time!"

"I'll tie your knot right," he grumbled, pulling as hard as he could on the line he'd just fastened down. He wouldn't dare say it too loud anymore.

"That'll do lads! Stay ready 'til lunch."

Thank goodness...

Wolflock sighed heavily and his whole body nearly collapsed from the immediate relief of being released from his duties. For three days he had been at the beck and call of Captain Blutro, in order to make up for the time they'd lost saving the mermaid Himi. Wolflock had to act as a crew member, and the captain seemed determined to work him to the bone. The crew laughed and said it was character building, but Wolflock resented every second. Having to learn ship terminology on the go was something he could have handled with ease but having to work as if he were a burly Corshman had worn his slender body out in just a few days.

He slumped off to lunch in the dining hall, where Mothy greeted him with bowls of salted vegetable stew and mushrooms. The dried vegetables were rehydrated in the hot water and, as he sipped the broth, his body felt restored. It was more rejuvenating than any magic potion and Wolflock's tired muscles thanked him for eating the two bowls.

"Having fun?" Mothy chuckled and passed him some buttered hemp seed bread.

Wolflock glared at him with half-lidded, exhausted eyes.

"It's a blast. A real hoot. Exactly how I wanted to

spend my trip through this freezing pond." He couldn't even muster any theatrical hand waving to exaggerate his point.

"Think of it this way," Mothy said through a mouthful of bread dipped in the stew, "you'll always know about boats, and you'll be fit for the climb up the mountain."

Ahh... yes... the mountain.

It was well known across all Puinteyle that new students at Mystentine University had to trek up the great mountain. It was the highest in the known world, and it required a guide to help avoid any dangers. After a thousand years, the path up to the university had become well walked, and very few people died on the journey anymore. It was more like a symbolic rite of passage nowadays.

Traders and beings living in Mystentine city often journeyed up to sell their wares to the students in the castle. Others came to receive medical treatments or have problems solved. Wolflock remembered his father sending off Huston, their driver, to go to Mystentine University to have a new harness developed that was more comfortable for the horses. They complained that the new, cheaper ones that flooded the Plugh market caused muscle aches and chaffing. Huston had come back with a lovely design that the horses adored, but it hadn't been beautiful enough, so Wolflock's father sent it to the artisans studying in the Shellinden Arts and History University to have it decorated.

This process took a lot longer and Wolflock remembered his father grumbling about artists not doing what he'd asked. Huston had enjoyed the journeys back and forth, and Wolflock had thought that he may have given the artisans the wrong information deliberately so he could travel. He had bluntly asked Huston if this was the case, to which Huston vehemently denied, but upon the next return from Shellinden, he returned with the correct and perfect design.

"Are you going to sleep, Lockie? You're not on the lunch shift, are you?" Mothy asked gently, laying a hand on Wolflock's aching arm.

He shook his head.

"I'll not be able to sleep from the pain. I don't want to miss the port either. We'll be on an even keel after Irid, so the movement will help me sleep."

"I think the captain enjoys having you out there, you know?"

Wolflock looked darkly at Mothy. "Torturing me, you mean?"

Mothy chuckled. "Well, that, and that you're a

pretty good worker when you're forced into it. The crew seem pretty happy too."

Wolflock pondered that echoing line in his mind for a while as he finished his meal and rested his aching bones in silence. The crew were jovial with him and treated him with a playful roughness they only reserved for each other during their downtime. He also couldn't think of when he'd heard the captain laugh more, even if it was at his expense.

To give himself just a few more moments of rest he ignored the heavy footsteps approaching.

"C'mon, mi'lad," Grogen sighed and clapped him on the shoulder. "We'll be pulling into Irid a'fore too long."

All pondering thoughts washed out of him as Wolflock groaned and dragged himself to his feet.

After a few hours of cruel labour later, Wolflock spotted it as he looked up from the new line he rearranged. Land. A split across the Northern horizon opened. At first it looked like an odd bluish cloud, a sliver of mist. Then it took form. A flat plain leading gradually up a hill into the edge of a crescent-shaped bay.

As the image solidified, he could see the deep green pine trees capped with snow gripping the slippery banks of mud and slush. Leafless trees clumped between the pines and surrounded a small town of log houses and grassy roofs. Many of the buildings were on stone stilts, sutured together with wooden walkways as the shifting silt washed in and out of the town's floor. Wolflock's piercing blue eyes fixed on the wharf, stretching out like a welcoming hand in the grey waters.

"Land ho!" Hognut cried from the crow's nest, causing a great stir as everyone ran forward to see the long-awaited land. It felt as if they had been in hibernation and were finally seeing the first rays of Spring just out ahead.

"Out fenders!" Blutro commanded from the wheel.

Drop the giant knotted cords to dangle over the side of the ship so the wharf doesn't scratch the ship. Gods help us if she's scratched.

His muscles instantly dulled their ache as he threw the giant knots over the ship, just in time to stop it from scratching the fine paintwork. His stomach, being light with elation, eased his pain and foul mood as the land was within reach. He could smell the mud, the wood smoke from pine being burnt. He could hear the chatter of the townsfolk, and he could even hear their boots on the ground.

"Out the boardwalk!"

He had never heard this command before, but he knew exactly what it meant.

Grogen and Geagle had it under control, though. While the others were tossing lines out for the wharf workers to tie off, Grogen and Geagle carried a long, large plank and rested it off the side of the ship.

The path to freedom!

It nearly glowed with happiness in the glittering sunbeams piercing through the clouds. The company stared at it with a palpable hunger. It had been over a fortnight since they'd touched land.

The ship finally stopped, held taut by the lines mooring it down. Slavidus stepped out in front of the boardwalk.

"Attention, everyone!" he boomed, holding out his list of passengers. "Before we depart for shore leave, I must implore you to be back on board before sunset. We will leave at sunset and no later. If you are not back on board before the sun has disappeared, we will have left you behind. No exceptions. Secondly, we say farewell to Faleen, Bleen, Froderyk, Fuhji, Tanni and Tinni. I'll let you ashore to say your merry parts and merry meets again."

They shed a few tears as they bundled their belongings. Wolflock didn't know why Goden and

Matroos had volunteered to take everyone's luggage off
the ship or why the other crew had groaned they hadn't
been selected until he saw the crew had to depart the ship
last unless they helped the passengers. As an honorary
member of the crew, he was also to stay on board until
each passenger leaving for land had departed.

"Quit yeh groanin', lad." Grogen tousled his black
hair, "Cap'in runs tha most polite ship tha' travels this far.
S'bad manners to let the crew off first."

Wolflock still persisted in grumbling until he saw
that the first passengers to scurry off the ship. Neither
giving nor receiving any farewells, Faleen and Bleen slunk
from the ship like the thieves of happiness they were.
During their recompense, he had requested the captain
station him nearby so he could monitor the changed
fortunes they told the affected crew and company. When
he wasn't available, Yifi stood in for him and diligently
corrected any offending language the twins used, much to
their chagrin.

While working as a crewman on the Silver Ice
Hair, Wolflock had found he had far more reason to be
social. People would often come and stand by him while
he laboured, offering him verbal support and stories that
kept his weary muscles from crying too loudly.

When he injured his forearm on his first day of

work, Nu and Stra had worked together to collect pepper, turmeric, and oil as a poultice for him, and he could work through the day regardless of the pain. Stra had checked up on him several times, chatting with Nu and learning about her medicines. The bald man was quite sharp and Wolflock felt he was an amicable acquaintance. He'd also leaned heavily on Grogen as a mentor, quickly becoming his ship's apprentice. For someone he initially thought was quite dull, Wolflock soon realised that for what Grogen lacked in book smarts, he made up for in worldly experience. Each unique passenger with marvellous stories gifted him a song to sing. Each trinket dangling off his person was a token for magnificent tasks he'd accomplished for his guests. Wolflock concluded Grogen was an extraordinarily blessed man, reflected in his not-so-naïve heart of gold.

His reminiscing thoughts were knocked out of him by a tiny missile wrapped around his middle.

"Merry Part, Wolflock!" Tinni wailed as he caught his breath.

"M-Merry part," he coughed and unwrapped her sticky, tiny arms.

"And merry meet again," her mother tittered behind her hand.

He nodded and returned the smile.

"Go on, Tinni. Ask him your question."

The tiny girl with auburn hair and reddish skin turned even redder as she let go of Wolflock and clung to her mother's arm.

"Umm..." She waved for her mother to come down so she could whisper into her ear.

Tanni giggled and nodded, holding her hair back. "Yes, that's good. Well done. Now you say it."

Wolflock raised an eyebrow and analysed them.

"Umm... Mr Wolflock, can I please practise my writing and send you letters at Mystentine?"

Tanni gave the little girl a nudge.

"Oh! If it is agreeable to you, sir."

"Uh..." He wasn't sure if he wanted to have the obligation of answering a child's letters, but she was very adventurous, so perhaps it could prove to be a diversion amongst his studies. Although it may detract from them as well. But what if the girl grew up to be a useful person? As he took his time to answer, her face dropped and he couldn't bear the awkward feeling that arose from her disappointment. "Of course you may. And I will answer as often as my studies will permit me to."

Her face split into a wide smile, and she gave him one more hug before Tanni embraced him as well.

"Thank you," she whispered to him before they

both departed.

As he watched them descend, he felt a clap on his shoulder. A familiar feeling, now, as all the crew had taken to smacking his shoulder as greeting, but not a familiar hand.

"Well, thanks for one of the more horrific, yet enlightening, travels I've been on," Froderyk laughed.

"You're welcome?"

"We'll send you a letter at the university when we've settled." Fuhji kissed his cheeks and gave his arms a squeeze. "Please keep Mothy safe."

"I can't promise anything, but I will do my best. It's more likely he'll keep me safe. Merry part."

"And merry meet again." Fuhji curtsied.

Froderyk placed his arm around her waist, and they left the ship, too.

Wolflock watched as each person stepped ashore. He'd spent over a month and a bit with these people, and they had quickly felt like family. He took up a seat on a crate by the mainmast and thought to himself about everything that had happened and all the cases he'd solved. The ship was bursting with mysteries asking to be discovered and a year on board couldn't be enough time to find them all.

Knowing he only had a few more days on the ship,

he lamented the lack of time he had to find them. He had sent Mothy hither and thither to find all the places he suspected to have secret compartments, doors, levers, and hidey holes, just to see if he was right. More often than not, he was.

He also had had no time to find the mysterious person with the knife. The one he suspected had tried to poison Mothy, kill Parihaan, and even himself. He only had a few clues, but nothing concrete. With a sigh, he resigned himself to never finding out who they may be. He didn't have the time, or the physical energy left to go hunting, especially for someone so dangerous.

"What a changed young man you have become," came a silky voice from his side.

Stra, the herbalist, stood and watched the luggage and stores being taken ashore with a satisfied smile. Wolflock could only assume he was as hungry for his feet on solid land as the rest of them were.

"Pardon?" Wolflock frowned at his comment.

"You're getting a tan from all this hard work. I must say it suits you."

"Now, now, Stra. Don't finish that thought because it most certainly doesn't suit me. I'm of gentile blood and hard work frustrates me because of the under-use of my mental faculties."

"Very well. I know someone telling you anything but what you want to be makes you violently ill," he raised his hands in surrender, "but all I will say is that the ship has been rather calm, with only Mr Mothy getting into any trouble. And his kind of trouble is more of the physical exploratory kind than your probing."

"He does crawl into all kinds of places, doesn't he?" Wolflock snorted, thinking of how Mothy had taken to swinging down from high places to land on his friend's shoulders while work on the ship distracted him.

"Has anyone properly thanked you for your efforts over the past month? I must say, being instrumental in the Quaretz twin's re-evaluation of their initial counsellings did much to distract the passengers over that boring crossing."

Wolflock bristled with pride at Stra's words. "No. The only thanks I received was to be indentured to the crew."

"Ah. Such a shame. Well, when you get off the ship, you and Mr Mothy should meet me at the little tea shop. My good friend owns it, and he has the most impeccable teas one has had the pleasure of sipping. There are muscle relaxants, mental acuity enhancers, and even a few magical ones. One time he made one that turned a woman's hair purple and curly for a few hours.

It was quite a sight."

Wolflock nodded as Stra spoke. Visiting a teahouse sounded intriguing, but he wasn't sure he wanted to be caught up inside and sitting for their few hours off board.

"I'm sure we can stop by for a while."

"Excellent! I'll have a tasting line ready."

The tall, thin, bald man bowed his head and departed the ship at the end of the line of passengers, eagerly stepping ashore.

"So, what are you waitin' for, Prince of the Rigging?" said a cheeky voice from behind him as a pair of hands almost shook him off his makeshift seat.

Wolflock caught himself and gave Mothy a shove, laughing. "Waiting for you to get your sorry sauce off the ship so I can leave. You're a passenger and I'm at your beck and call."

"Well, best I get moving then?" Mothy grinned from ear to ear and began moving as slowly as possible with exaggerated swimming motions.

Wolflock growled and chased him to the gangplank, where the captain caught them both by the collars.

"Oi! No running along here, boys. You'll fall in the water and catch the death of you. Now go slow, Mr

Enitnelav. I'll have no tomfoolery in town, either. You come back to this ship as respectable as you left."

"But Captain," Mothy drawled in a long slow voice, "that would mean I come back with no respect at all."

The captain gave him a warning stare, making Mothy laugh nervously and scurry down the way, Wolflock's shirt still grasped in the captain's fist. Now that Mothy was off the plank surely he'd let him go.

"While we're away, Mr Felen, I expect you to take a close stock of all remaining cargo on each floor and report back to me with what we need to restock in Creast. Then the linen needs washing. Matroos and Goden will be back with the new soapwort soon. That will need to be cleaned, soaked, and strained. Then bottled and stored in the pantry and hull."

"Sure. When I get back, I'll-"

"When you get back?"

Wolflock's gut sank.

"No shore leave for you today, lad. Most of the crew only have an hour before they have to come back and hasten away. You're to guard the ship. Particularly from any sparrows or rats trying to sneak aboard. And of anyone passing to Creast without permission."

Wolflock's shoulders slumped. "But Captain! It's been so long. Can't I just spend a little bit of time ashore?

I have letters to send!"

Captain Blutro clapped his shoulder and leaned in close. "You're not going to receive or send letters from Irid. It's too far out of the way. Post them in Creast and they'll get there a month faster. If I didn't believe this was for your own safety, I would let you and your friends run amok all day and still let you come back late. Do this for me, lad, and I'll let you steer the ship when we hit the ice."

It didn't really sound worth it, but Wolflock knew better than to argue with the captain. He argued with everyone else, but, after he fought with the captain about the placement of the ties and was nearly thrown overboard, he learned that Captain Blutro saw things no one else did. Wolflock bit his lip and huffed, turning away, and vowing to himself that, when all this was said and done, he would have the captain write him a letter to answer all his questions about his journey on the Silver Ice Hair.

Captain Blutro released his collar, and Wolflock slouched away with a dejected sigh.

"I am sorry, Wolflock."

He looked up to see Nu with her shining black hair tucked under a thick furry hood. She looked like a mountain princess with her fluffy gloves and embroidered belt.

"It's not your fault, Nu. I will just waste away on the deck for a few more days. If it was anyone but Captain saying it, I would have just ignored them."

"Would it make you happy to have a gift brought back for you?"

"If you can find a good cobbler, get me their details. Besides that, maybe a local dish or drink. Something warm though. The cold is getting very bitey."

"I have never had cold bite, but I understand. Warm treats."

"Nothing too sweet, though!" he called as she walked to the gangplank.

She turned and rolled her eyes at him with a smile. "You think I do not know what flavours you like by now? Nothing sweet, nothing sickly, nothing that makes your mind cloudy. I will find you something very good."

Wolflock gave her a rueful smile and shuffled to his duties. He couldn't help but feel like the captain had deliberately given him an excessive number of tasks to stop him from snooping, yet he'd unwittingly given him the one task he needed to do exactly that.

As he took stock in the hull, he opened every crate, every unlocked chest, every barrel, checking the contents, logging the resources, and making sure he categorised everything perfectly. Then, he moved to the crew quarters, taking stock of the cleaning equipment, broken instruments, and the polish used to keep the ship in perfect shape. He was glad that, in the logbook, Slavidus had a clear code for each item, which meant he could duplicate the process, making it faster. If he finished his duties, he might help Matroos and Goden haul the soapwort back on board and get at least to the wharf.

He made his way to the passenger cabins and collected all the linen baskets sitting just inside the doors. Orders were to dress down everyone's rooms today and restore them with fresh sheets and towels by the time they got back at sunset.

Wolflock had come to realise that the Silver Ice Hair crew were trained to be far more subtle than he had thought was possible for such large folk. Now he knew that, during the organised suppers, activities, and sleep, maintenance took place away from the public eye to uphold a professional image of the ship and crew. While passengers were completely off the ship, it could receive a much needed deep clean and check over, without interruption. That included the bedrooms. They completely stripped the empty rooms, cleansed, and checked for lost objects, gifts, and hidden away items.

The twins had left a nasty-looking poppet of

Wolflock under the bed, which he dismantled and threw the parts out of the window, dusting his hands of their last, poor effort to magically sabotage him. They'd also left behind old incense stick ends and ash from something. Perhaps a burnt letter, judging by the grey flakes. Wolflock stripped their bedding and went about his work, glad that they could never strike at him again.

Froderyk and Fuhji had left nothing behind except for strands of hair and a bin full of crumpled letters from Fuhji trying to tell her parents she was with child. Tanni and Tinni had left behind a little dolly made of seashells and wool. It looked terrible, so Wolflock assumed Tinni had made it, but the gesture was meant to be sweet, so he set it on Grogen's bed with a small note explaining where it was from. Grogen would be the one to appreciate such a gesture more than anyone else, as he possessed a childlike heart.

Wolflock had to leave a note about the doll because, depending on the various cultures in Puinteyle, dolls, poppets and effigies could be used for good or ill. Some people, like the twins, could make a doll that brought sickness, ill fortune, or other forms of back luck to the subject. Other dolls could cure illness, bless a person and their house, or bring various forms of good luck to them. Sometimes dolls were just made to be played with or because the person had a crafty hand. It was safer to be careful with each form than take them for granted.

He saved Parihaan's room for last. He always did this. Whenever the Captain had him on any room duties, he would stop last there so he could speak with her for a moment and have a break. His hands were too sore to play the violin, but he still told her about his day and the goings on around the ship. She was still under constant surveillance from himself, Mothy, Geagle, and Haatji. Sometimes Yifi and Slavidus would sit with her on their off time, too. She had moved and groaned, which Nu assured them was a grand sign.

He came to her room and rolled her off her old sheets and onto fresh ones smelling of lavender and pine. Before he put the old sheets into the linen basket, he sighed, leaning against her wardrobe at the end of her bed.

"We're nearly there. At Creast, I mean. This has been such a long journey, Parihaan. I've never come to call so many people by their first names. I know it's only been a month and a bit, but it feels like this journey has taken five years. It's nice for it to be ending. When you wake up, I hope it's still fine for me to address you by your first name. We've spoken about so much and yet so little. I still wonder if we'll ever meet in a conscious state."

He took a few deep, slow breaths, contemplating what it would be like to speak with her as a person and what it would be like to live off the ship once more. Even the ship just remaining so still, nestled up against the pier, felt alien to him.

"Parihaan is fine."

The hoarse whisper startled him so much he leapt to the door. He turned to see the light brown eyes of Parihaan looking down past her nose at him. For a moment, he thought she was still unconscious, but then she blinked.

"You're awake?" he gasped, falling to his knees beside her bed. Instinctively, he grasped her hand laying on the fresh blankets. She still felt quite cool.

"Mmm..." she hummed, watching him as if it took all her effort to keep her eyes open.

Her throaty hum crackled, so he reached for some water and carefully pressed the cup to her dry lips. She took a few sips and turned her head, closing her eyes.

"This is remarkable. I-I-I'm so pleased you're awake."

Parihaan kept her eyes closed, but her hand gripped his with the strength of fog, letting him know she was still awake.

"Thank you," she wheezed.

Her face relaxed and her hand went limp in his. For a few more moments he waited, watching her breathe evenly, before he left the room, numb to the core, and closed the door behind him. He wished Nu would come back soon so he could understand what had just happened. His mind whirled with the stare in her brown eyes and the conscious movement she'd managed. He had to tell someone.

But who? The potential murderer was still part of the crew and company. If anyone found out she was awake, her life would be in even more danger. The fiend may get desperate enough to silence her. He decided to tell the Captain, Mothy and Nu. Geagle wouldn't be able to keep the secret, but at least the other three could help him devise a plan to keep her safe until Creast. Until then, he would check on her between every task and make sure she was getting what she needed.

For the rest of the day, Wolflock forgot to lament being unable to set foot on land. He let Matroos and Goden know he thought he saw Parihaan move, so he had to check on her often, which allowed him to leave intermittently without fear of being told off. In between laundry and prepping the soapwort solution, Wolflock kept an anxious eye on the gangplank for his friends.

Parihaan stayed asleep for most of the day, waking only to take a bit of soup and another cup of water. Her throat was so dry and so out of use that it was hard for her to speak, but she smiled at Wolflock and gestured with the pressure of her olive hand on his for what she needed.

He confessed that at one point he thought she would wake up and be as volatile as before, but she responded with a raspy, "I could hear everything."

That alone spoke volumes to him, making him feel both embarrassed and relieved. She didn't speak again until the crew and company had returned, and the ship had cast off. Wolflock caught Mothy boarding with a scroll of paper as Captain Blutro and Slavidus discussed a large order of fish from Irid to Creast.

"Mothy! Parihaan! You need to... what is that?"

"Oh, this?" Mothy smirked, smacking the roll of paper in his hand. "This is a legal document for the captain."

"What?"

Mothy's smile widened as he unrolled it. "The Duke of Irid hereby states that for such a wildly entertaining performance of acrobatics and humour, I do declare that Mr Mothy Enitnelav has gained an insurmountable modicum of respect and privilege in this town. Furthermore, the respect shall only be permitted to be maintained while Mr Enitnelav remains on Irid soil and shall be dispersed whence he returns to water."

Captain Blutro frowned, "You... went to bother the duke for paperwork saying..."

"Yes, Captain. I have returned with the exact same amount of respect as I left with, by order of the duke. Who, I must say, has the most delightful little mini snow dogs I've ever seen."

Mothy strutted past them in an exaggerated walk. Wolflock supposed his friend thought a respectful lord would walk like and made it to the stairs before turning on his heel and racing back. He pulled a fluffy ball from his pocket and pushed it into his hands.

"There's a hundred types of hair in that. Figure it out because the duke couldn't, and neither could the local witch."

Wolflock blinked, holding the fluffy sphere, and watched as Mothy shot back across the deck and down the stairs, leaving him and the captain to glance at each other in shock.

"Uh... Right then. Hop to, Wolflock. Time to cast off!"

The company descended below deck with their new purchases from the town of Irid, warming up while dinner was being prepared.

"In fenders!"

Pull in the giant knotted cords.

"Cast off!"

Pull away from the wharf.

"Hoist sails!"

And they were off again. The gentle rocking of the ship made Wolflock feel oddly at home, and, even though his muscles still ached, he knew what had to be done to get the ship to sail smoothly now.

"We'll hit the ice in the hour! Prepare the wings!"

Prepare the... what?

Wolflock felt that sense of accomplishment and comfortable knowledge slip out from under his feet.

"Grogen! What-"

"Follow my lead, mi'lad!" he chortled and began moving around the giant silver wings on the side of the ship.

The crewman untied ropes and buckles that held down large boxes, revealing that they weren't containing stores, but huge gears and shiny machinery. Wolflock helped bundle the ropes and finally they moved the box to reveal a great machine attached to the metal silver wings on the sides of the ship.

"Cap'in's great pa built these on the ship," Grogen grinned at Wolflock's amazement at the gears and mechanisms glittering in the sunrise. "He didn't want to destroy the ice. It took so much more effort ta do tha, and he liked the way it looked. This... well... Just watch."

Grogen heaved the lever to the machine with a clunk. He pushed with all his muscles to turn the crank as metal squealed in excitement. At the same time, Geagle did the same, bringing the leaver to three quarters of the way to the water racing beside the ship. As he did, the giant silver wings swung forward and angled at a fifty-degree angle to the water, catching the spray and glistening like the hungry jaw of a shark.

"Steady, men!" Captain Blutro shouted, and Wolflock watched over the side of the ship as it raced towards the white ice before them.

"Steady..."

It was getting closer and closer. Surely the ship would cut into the new icy land and then just come to a halt.

"Grab hold, laddy!" Grogen grunted and yanked him closer to help with the crank.

Wolflock did as he was told and wrapped his hands around the smooth metal bar. The ship struck the ice and shattered it at its edge. A jolt shook the ship, punctuating the calm with a grating, crunching and cracking noise as it ground its way through the white and blue slab of frost. The ship slowed and Wolflock thought that maybe the wings were about to cut the ice, but then Captain Blutro shouted out.

"Drop the wings!"

The L shaped silver wings hit the ice and Wolflock felt the ship lurch a bit, grateful to be hanging onto the crank, but it didn't feel like it did significant damage to the floor of ice before them.

"Slack the windward brace! Hoist all sails!"

Hoist ALL the sails!?

Wolflock knew that was an odd thing since they'd been on a winding river and then a choppy sea, but clearly the ship needed all its power for something.

"Push the wings forward!" Captain Blutro shouted as the ship groaned and moved forward, its nose dipping and water spraying lightly over the ship.

Grogen, Wolflock, and Geagle shoved at the same time and the ship rose out of the water and onto the thick ice. The strength the crew held amazed Wolflock, and how beautifully made the ship's machinery was. The multitude of gears gave the wings more leverage, and it took less effort to move the ship up onto them.

In his awe at the machinery, he hardly noticed when Grogen slipped off the handle.

"Grogen!" Captain Blutro shouted.

Wolflock dove forward without thinking and caught the long handle, stopping it from slipping as the ship moved lopsidedly forward, swinging around back towards the watery ocean. Even with his total strength, the bar kept crushing him closer to the deck. Slavidus was by his side in an instant and threw his shoulder against the bar, shoving with him. With their combined effort they got it back to a vertical position before Grogen got back to his feet and pulled from the opposite direction, evening out the listing ship.

"All the way, lads!" Captain Blutro called out, and the ship finally locked the wings down. "Now lock wings."

Grogen panted and wedged the lever into a hook that held it steady, avoiding catching anyone's eye.

Slavidus and Wolflock watched him even when his face flushed. The giant man looked embarrassed, rubbing his hands as if his knuckles hurt.

"Slavidus... I'm..."

"It's arthritis, isn't it?" Wolflock frowned and stepped forward, looking at Grogen's bulging knuckles.

"I can still do me work!" Grogen growled.

Slavidus stepped in front of Wolflock and pushed down Grogen's hands.

"I know you can. We all do. Don't think of it."

Grogen nodded and walked away, helping to lead

lines from the main sails up to the wheel so the captain could control the ship without the rudder being used. Wolflock looked uncomfortably at Slavidus.

"He'll not be able to work on the ship if his hands are injured... Will he?"

Slavidus shook his head.

"This is a big ship. It needs sturdy folk working on her. Grogen will be fine though. We'll keep getting him medicine as we travel. He'll have his retirement."

"How old is Grogen?" Wolflock frowned. With his immense body and bushy beard, Wolflock couldn't determine his age at all.

Slavidus scratched his chin thoughtfully, "About fifty something summers I'd say. I don't rightly know , though."

"Lockie!" Wolflock turned just in time to get barrelled by Mothy with Nu in tow. "Come! Come look!"

Wolflock shook his head a little as his friend dragged him by the sleeve to the front of the ship to see it glide smoothly along the perfect flat ice. The view was stunning. Dying sunlight made the world pink and the ice still gleamed with yellow and blue slashes of colour. Little mounds where the ice had flaked and built up were demolished in spectacular explosions as the ship streamed along.

Wolflock felt so at ease by the sight. There was no bumping, no swaying, just a clear, smooth journey. Some seals and mermaids dived into holes they'd dug into the ice, but besides that, the sea was simply a glowing orb of light and colour.

"You didn't tell me she was awake!" Mothy hissed, his voice low in the beautiful quiet of the magical landscape around them.

"I tried to. Don't let anyone else know yet. We have to tell the captain and decide on what we're going to do."

"I will take care of her." Nu nodded with a stern resolution.

"She is in the best hands then."

"Oi..." Mothy whined and nudged Wolflock's arm.

After a short laugh, they fell quiet, taking in the view before them as the sun sank behind them. The wind whistled past them and they stayed silent for a long time before the captain called Wolflock away to work again. The new scenery had given him more energy, but he tried to take his duties at the front of the ship to take it all in.

Mothy and Nu stood to the side as the ship glided into the night. Wolflock had grown quite fond of the three of them being together, and their adventures had filled many letters to his sister. As the ship steadied into the new form, the captain allowed the crew to relax. Much like the slower night sailing, the crew only needed a lookout and a few people to help the ship sail across the ice with ease. Wolflock took the chance to tell the Captain about Parihaan and his shoulders slumped with relief.

"That is great news, lad. Let's see if she's up for a few questions, and then we'll let the company know."

"But won't that put her in danger, Captain?"

Captain Blutro frowned and thought for a moment. "No. I don't believe it will. She will become somewhat of a celebrity over the next few days, I'm sure. Everyone will want to speak to her and that company, along with your guardianship and that of our fellow watchers, will keep her safe. If we were to keep this private, she is likely to have an accident that will be unexplained. What say you?"

"That is sound reasoning. Very well. You may speak to her when Nu clears her for discussion."

Captain Blutro raised an eyebrow and sighed. "Thank you, Mr Felen, for permission to see my own passenger on my ship."

Three days passed and Wolflock became quite accustomed to the exercise of running the ship. The captain took quite a bit of glee, watching him take command. At first, Wolflock corrected the knots around the ship, as distinct lines required different knots. Then he began finding who had tied them wrong and (with Mothy's guidance) showed them the error of their ways. His muscles stopped aching, and he became bossier and bossier as he felt better. In order to keep the crew sane, Captain Blutro sent him up to the crow's nest with Mothy, Nu, or a crew member at all times where he watched like a hawk for hours for fauna and icebergs to avoid.

He got little opportunity to speak with Parihaan, but he found out that she loved his music and felt as if they had become fast friends from his discussions. She was a locked vault for what each person had discussed with her in private, but also said she had no clear recollection of anything that occurred while she was intoxicated from the Krieger Zwerg dock to when she fell down the stairs.

One of the most remarkable things to develop was Haatji and Parihaan's friendship. When they saw one another awake, both burst into tears and hugged one another as if they were long-lost sisters. Nu said that Haatji barely left Parihaan's side, constantly grooming, feeding, and performing acts of service for the woman. None of them were sure if it was a way of atoning for her part in Parihaan's fall or if they kindled their new friendship from an understanding developed through their time together.

There was a sense of community and importance amongst the ship's crew that Wolflock thoroughly enjoyed. He wasn't accustomed to anyone but his immediate family welcoming him, and having a feeling of acceptance and comradery around him brought feelings of comfort he'd never known. The crew all tolerated him and found his behaviour quite endearing, knowing they only had to play along for a few days, but they couldn't deny they were happy to see him away in the crow's nest entertaining Mothy and Nu. They could often hear the theatrics from the deck, and, several times, thought the boys were going to topple out of the giant basket.

In celebration of their final evening together, Wolflock fiddled, Mothy drummed and Grogen sang while the crew and company danced into the late hours of the night. The children could stay up late and Nu and Haatji helped Parihaan come up to enjoy the festivities. She looked so thin and sickly, barely able to stand on her own, but her eyes were clear, and she could feel her legs again. Geagle doubly celebrated that Parihaan may walk again one day and cradled her in a slow dance, making her giggle like a child.

The evening drew on and the captain began telling tales to help the children fall asleep.

"What tales do you have of Creast?" Mothy asked, resting his arm on the bodhrán.

"Ah. Creast. The town of mermaids and jewels." Captain Blutro leaned back in his seat, gazing out into the starry sky. "We are very lucky we'll be arriving tomorrow, because soon will be the Pisces Moon."

The remaining crew and company fell silent to listen intently.

"It is known that mermaids love shiny things. Beautiful jewels in particular. Well, many hundreds of years ago, the people in Creast were starving, and they knew not what to do. They had been gifted a giant sapphire with two crystal fish swimming inside it from an evil wizard who wanted them to starve. For all their food and livestock, he traded them this gem. As the people suffered, he laughed, but the mermaids of the bay loved the gem. When a young fisher saw this, they threw the gem into the water, pleading with the mermaids to help save the town. The full moon shone down through the water and the stars were perfectly aligned to please the mermaids. They rushed to the gemstone and drove the fish to the bay, saving the town."

The listeners released the collective breath from

the relief of a happy ending to the story.

"Today, Creast upholds the Pisces Moon tradition whether or not they need it because they're then able to send the dried fish to smaller settlements through the bitter Winter. That full moon is upon us tomorrow night and you will all be able to see the full beauty of merfolk and land folk working together."

The group rested in the story's ambience for longer before Grogen sang a low tune in native Shirth. Wolflock didn't know what it meant, but he was sure it had something to do with the captain's tale. After a few more slow songs, everyone but Mothy, Wolflock and Captain Blutro had retired for the night. The boys climbed up into the crow's nest with a blanket each and watched the frosty night glowing with green and blue lights from the mystical ice.

They did not need to speak, but just enjoyed the serenity of the ship gliding across the thick ice until the grey of dawn welcomed them back into the water.

On the final morning, there was an eerie silence as Wolflock sat on the edge of the crow's nest. His fiddle was in hand, but he wasn't playing. His gut trembled, but it wasn't from the salty preserved breakfast, and he couldn't keep his eyes off the horizon. Something in his gut told him he needed to keep searching in the grey light of dawn along that line.

Then... there it was.

A thin glimpse of bluish mist that looked more like mist than land appeared before them. It grew taller and taller and the outline of trees along the banks turned the blueness into black.

"It's there! It's there! Creast! It's Creast!"

No one below him seemed to respond except for Grogen, who looked up with a raised bushy eyebrow.

"Tha's not the command, laddy!" He chortled.

Wolflock grinned and cupped his hands around his mouth.

"LAND HO!"

Rhiannon D. Elton

CHAPTER 2

Merry Part

Wolflock's shouts woke the ship, bringing even the weariest folk to the top deck for the much-anticipated final stop. Grogen climbed up the rigging with a flask of hot tea for them. Unable to take their eyes off the misty land, becoming more solid as the ship sailed closer, they unscrewed the flasks and let the first wisps of steam snake out.

"Yeh jus' wait." Grogen hung off the edge of the crow's nest, taking a swig out of his own flask. "Tha Creast Bay is magical, yeh hear. Waters as blue as the Spring sky and a giant sapphire. It's said tha if yeh touch the sapphire yeh'll have all kinds a good luck."

"Have you ever touched it?" Mothy asked, drumming his hands excitedly on the burly sailor's hairy arm.

"Oh, a couple-a times. When I was a youngin' I got dared by a local lass tha I couldn't do it and I bet 'er a hot dinner I could. Damn near drowned a'cause it was high tide, but I touched that gem and thought I pushed it over when I kicked off it ta get me breath again. And another time was a few years later; I went ta git one of our old crewmate's engagement ring and thought I'd give it a slap on my way through. Old Betty couldn' swim even a doggy paddle, poor sod. Left the ship when she married Mr Butterfingers, but I can' judge."

The captain didn't call for Wolflock or Grogen to come down, hustling the rest of the crew to assist with the docking. Wolflock expected to see glittering blue waters with crystalline ripples as Grogen had conveyed.

But, as the ship pulled into the bay and bumped against the fenders and the dock, a confused and disappointed hush fell over them. No doubt the rest of the company had been regaled with similar stories of the bay's beauty, but, under the cloudy sky, the murky brown waters were uninspiring.

"Wha' on Pelaia..." Grogen mumbled to himself, his

bushy brow furrowed in concern. "Wha's this then?"

"It doesn't always look like this?" Wolflock pinched his chin between his index finger and thumb.

"I ain't never seen it like this afore. I best go 'elp with the cargo, boys. Sorry 'bout the bay. Don' yeh get inta anymore trouble without me around ta save yeh, yeh hear?"

Before either could respond, he was down the stiff rigging. Wolflock's eyes scanned the bay, seeing the much smaller ships along the wharf and two larger, wider ships anchored further out to sea. The dark blue water that stretched for a few miles before the ice formed distinctly outlined the edge of the brown water. There was a current keeping the brown water stuck in the bay.

Curious...

He couldn't sit with his thoughts for too long as Slavidus walked over the deck barking orders.

"You've had your fun, now. Everyone, back to their cabins. We're checking off everything. Your luggage will be delivered off the ship where you can collect it. As I check you off, you can request it be delivered to your carriage or accommodation. Back to your cabins now."

Mothy and Wolflock descended from the crow's nest, grinning around at the hasty crew.

"That goes for you two as well. Back to your rooms."

"Don't you still need me for deck duties?" Wolflock

asked with a sly smirk.

Slavidus raised his eyebrow and looked up at the captain. "Oi! Captain? Is Mr Felen still employed?"

Captain Blutro chuckled, hooking the Silver Ice Hair wheel to keep it steady. "Only if you really want to haul crates and trunks onto the dock for the next few hours."

"I shall be off then!" Wolflock laughed, turned on his heel and ran down the stairs to pack his things.

Most of the other company had packed their belongings and were talking from their doors across the hall. Mothy brought his single bag into Wolflock's room and laid on his bed while the dark-haired boy folded his clothes and combed his hair.

"Free at last!" he sighed, shutting his trunk with a snap.

"Don't lie, you liked it. You were so diligent with your work and not for a moment did you act like you were going to surrender. Even through all your complaining."

"Surrender? It never came to my attention that it was an option, my dear Mothy."

The nervousness sprinkled through the air washed over them as they could finally leave the ship via the gang plank. Slavidus checked them off by name and handed them a receipt of travel. Mothy scrunched his receipt into his pocket, but Wolflock looked over it. The unique and intricate border, as well as an ancient sigil for blessing travels, just showed him even more that the Silver Ice Hair had been a ship of the highest-grade service right from start to finish, minus a few hiccups.

"One case, one trunk, and one Mr Felen. Merry part, lad." Slavidus nodded a last goodbye before glancing at Yifi. She hugged Geagle farewell and Slavidus' face twitched with an expression that looked like fear.

"And merry meet again, First Mate. I must say, though," he added and flicked Slavidus' clipboard to get his full attention, "I expect you won't need me as a crewmate any longer because you'll soon have another joining. I'd say one journey to Shellinmerth and back and she'll send her resume in."

"I... How... She didn't..." Slavidus stuttered.

"Considering the only time I saw her in her room this past week was to write her resume, it may very well be sooner. Check her wastebin, man. You'll see."

Slavidus' astonishment dissolved into amusement as he laughed and shook his head. "I know you well enough now, Mr Felen, that you, of all people, would know our plans even before we do. Please stay out of trouble, though."

"I make no promises that fate won't let me keep." Wolflock shrugged and slung his bag over his shoulder, taking his first step onto the gangplank and down onto the broad wharf.

Wolflock didn't anticipate how hard stepping off the Silver Ice Hair would be. He hadn't set foot on land in three weeks, and the exhilaration of finally being on sturdy ground made him numb. This was it. He was one huge step closer to independence. No longer being chaperoned by anyone his family deemed fit for him. He wasn't being parented by the captain or crew. This was unadulterated freedom. He was stepping out alone.

It was terrifying.

The gang plank creaked as he moved down it. A tattooed man peddling a stone and wooden machine craned the larger crates, boxes, barrels, and heavy objects down onto the pier. Wolflock thought the machine had to be far too heavy to move like the dock worker was, but his tattoos moved along his arms and legs and reinforced his movements.

"Fascinating..." he nodded to himself. "To work such a large machine alone. Much like my journey."

Without looking, he stepped to the firm dock. He had a moment of alarm when he felt nothing under his foot, but Mothy caught him in a tight hug.

"We made it! Lockie! We made it! Haha!"

He hurled Wolflock around in a circle before setting

him back on his dizzy feet.

Not entirely alone.

The dock was a bustle of activity, not only because the Silver Ice Hair had docked but also because of the Creast locals putting up long wreaths of evergreen plants and flowers around the bay. Although the piers and boardwalks coming out from the bay were wooden on top, the beams holding it above the water were pillars of stone. The crescent-shaped shore was lined with a ten-foot stone retaining wall, cluttered by all manner of little stalls selling trinkets to travellers, dockworkers, and fishers. The tide was low, giving off a pungent seaweed stench that mixed with the drying meat and wood smoke. Wolflock spotted a group of children sloshing through the soft sand at the base of the wall, lifting buckets to a sparkling little stall. They certainly had the biggest throng of onlookers, and he wanted to see what was so special about their business.

Torn between racing over to satiate his curiosity and letting Mothy say farewell to the people he was so fond of, Wolflock waited on the edge of the group. He wouldn't admit to anyone, even himself, that he didn't feel right leaving without saying goodbye to a few people as well.

"How long is everyone staying in Creast?" He tugged on his friend's sleeve as Mothy hugged Matroos.

"Captain says a few days. We got nearly our whole

week back thanks to your extra work, Wolflock," Matroos smiled as he clapped Wolflock's shoulder. "It will give the water some time to freeze, and we'll have a fast, smooth journey back to the river."

"Glad I could help. Maybe next time I'll just steer."

Matroos chuckled darkly. "Thinking you'll cause enough trouble again on your return journey? Do me a favour, Wolflock?"

"Aye?"

"Try to stay out of trouble or try to not get caught."

Wolflock shrugged as Matroos moved on to say goodbye to Veluse.

"Let me know if you see Nu, aye? We have to say a merry part to her at least." Mothy craned his neck around to spot the Nan family.

"Wolflock? Mothy?" came a quiet voice from behind them.

The boys turned to see Parihaan being gently seated on one of the chairs from the dining hall by Geagle.

"Parihaan! How are you feeling?"

She smiled and drew her head scarf around her black hair for warmth, nodding a thanks to Geagle.

"Y-yes! The chair! I'll fetch it!" he stammered and ran off.

"Chair?" Mothy asked.

Wolflock scanned over her. "A wheeled chair. Geagle is off to find you one, isn't he?"

She nodded, looking down from them. "He's been very kind to me. You all have. I wanted to apologise for the trouble I put you through. It has been a long time since anyone showed me that level of care, let it be so many people all at once. I wish I had time to repay it."

"There's no need," Mothy waved her statement away.

"I wanted to ask if I may write to you when I'm settled at my cousins? Haatji pressed me for my details, and I realised I don't remember the address."

"How has your memory been?" Wolflock asked quickly, squatting down to be eye level with her.

She shook her head. "I remember bits and pieces of what was spoken to me. Music and the sound of thunder. I remember things from my childhood and my early years... not much, if anything, from when I had... from when I had taken drink."

Mothy sat by her and offered his hand to comfort her. She took it as she drew a deep breath to steady herself.

"Well, our address will be Mystentine University. Nice and simple. Can't miss it. Big mountain and straight up to the top." Mothy laughed.

"You're welcome to write to both of us at any time.

We'll respond whenever we're able."

"Thank you. That means quite a lot to me. Oh! Here comes Geagle. I thought he would be much slower than that."

Geagle came running back with a soft chair attached to four wheels and, without another word, transferred Parihaan into it with all the tenderness he could muster. He smiled sweetly at the woman and then seemed to remember himself, snatching up the dining room chair and running back up the gangplank to return it.

"Merry part, Mothy. Merry part, Wolflock."

"And merry meet again, Parihaan."

She tested out her new chair, rolling over to the captain across the smooth stone road. Yifi, Haatji and Veluse accosted Wolflock, all wanting lengthy 'merry part's. He decided that the next time he had to have any kind of separation from an intimate group, he would sneak away and leave them notes, for this was drawing out far beyond his liking.

After what felt like an hour of lengthy farewells, he spotted a shining black haired head poke out from around a crate.

"Mothy!" He hissed in excitement for his friend.

Mothy looked at him and he nodded toward the black hair. Mothy went to step towards the place Wolflock nodded, but he froze.

"Go on. Go speak to her," Wolflock nudged him onwards.

The blond boy bit his lip and hesitated, but, with another push, Wolflock moved him closer.

"Keep an eye out for Nan Ji and the boys?"

"If they aren't behind the crate?"

"I... hmm... Nope. I can't do it."

Mothy tried to walk away, but Wolflock hooked his arm and marched him over to the boxes. Nu sat amongst the trunks, craning her neck around to the roads heading away from the docks, looking out for something.

A silent battle occurred between the boys as Wolflock tried to move Mothy into Nu's vision. Finally, Wolflock's stubbornness won out.

"I thought you were serious about her!"

"I am!"

"Then, what are you afraid of?"

"I don't want to be parted!"

"Then just say 'merry meet again', you fool! If you don't, you'll be parted, anyway. At least this way you'll have the promise of seeing each other again."

With a final shove, Mothy knocked into the box Nu sat behind.

"Mothy?"

Wolflock snorted with laughter and crossed his arms, keeping an eye out for anyone who would interrupt.

"I... Nu... Umm..."

"I am so happy I got to see you."

"Uhh... are you staying for the festival tonight?"

Wolflock kept them in the corner of his vision, and he saw her shake her head.

"Baba is needed for an urgent case in Corsh. We must head there in the next hour with all our supplies. He is getting a caravan as we speak."

"Oh..." a long silence made Wolflock worried his friend wouldn't say what he needed to, but then Mothy spoke again. "I'm going to miss you."

Nu took his hand. "I am going to miss you, too. You have been a good friend to me."

"When I finish my studies, I would like to meet again. I've... I have never met anyone like you."

"Mothy... I would like that more than anything. I cannot promise what you want, though."

"I'm not asking for any promises, Nu. I just want to know you'll be happy to see me when I do visit. I'm going to become a doctor, you know? Maybe I could work at your clinic in Xiayah."

"My clinic? You mean my father's clinic?"

Mothy took her other hand and drew closer. "No.

Your clinic."

Wolflock saw a fast motion between them and when he glanced back, he saw them both in a passionate embrace. He looked away quickly and swallowed.

"Please take this. It's a way for us to always stay connected. I have the sister opal and, when we're close, it will glow."

Wolflock glanced back to see him giving her a hand carved wooden flower.

"A dandelion. This is beautiful. Thank you. Please take this." She drew the hair comb from her long black hair and pressed it into his hands. "It is not a gift. You must give it back one day."

"I promise."

Wolflock watched the street corner and saw Didi race past with a stick in his hand as he swatted at the seagulls.

"Psst! They're coming."

The pair separated, looking sheepish.

"Well, Nu, it's been enlightening, and I wish you the best. Merry part." Wolflock turned and shook her hand as if the three of them had been talking for quite some time.

"Ahem. And you as well, Lockie. Merry meet again."

Gege jogged up to them, panting, "Nu! We... got... the... carts."

"Excellent. Did father haggle a good price?"

"No, but they will discount the use of them if the owner's morning sickness medicine works."

Nu buried her arms in the herb bags and began passing things out to her brother.

"We'll leave you to it," Wolflock said as he steered Mothy away. His friend moved as if he were floating on a cloud. He tried to avoid Nan Ji, but, somehow, he caught them.

"Well, boys. It has been a journey. If you are ever in Shruiken, come and find us at the most prestigious clinic in Xiayah. Merry part," he said, puffing out his chest.

"We shall indeed. And merry meet again," Wolflock said a touch coldly and shook the man's long fingered hand.

Nan Ji shook Mothy's hand, but held it for too long, scrutinising his scarlet face and open mouth. Wolflock flicked Mothy's chin, making him close his gaping maw, and dragged his friend to their belongings.

As they returned to their possessions, Mothy stared after Nu, watching the Nan family get into their carriage together.

"I think I'm in love, Lockie."

Wolflock rolled his eyes and dug through his trunk to find a jacket to ward off the bitter sea breeze.

"If you love a person, you're bound to die. If you love your work, you'll live eternal."

"That's poetic. Don't know what it means, but it sounds callous."

"It means," Captain Blutro chuckled as he strode up to them, "you're better off loving your work and only your work if you want to never change."

"I never thought of death as a change, Captain. More of an ending."

"That's not a change? Such as this ending here. I wanted to let you know a few things before you disappeared from my guardianship forever."

Wolflock put his jacket on and stood at attention.

"Firstly, I want to thank you again for the pains you took aboard my ship to set certain things right. Aujin also offers his thanks. Secondly, I wanted to thank you for keeping me in... well, a better place when my prejudices reared their heads. I have a far clearer idea for how to deal with things, such as smuggling from within the ship now. You've also brought hours of entertainment and good work to the ship, albeit, you've also damaged significant amounts of property. I think we're all balanced from that and those."

Mothy and Wolflock smirked at one another.

"Lastly, I wanted to let you know that, although your assistance over the last week was very helpful, it was not why

I had you work under my supervision at that time. Locking you away in your room would have prevented mischief just the same."

"I know, I know. It was to teach me some wonderful life lessons. You tradesfolk always think calloused hands are akin to depth of personality."

"Wolflock!" Mothy gasped.

Captain Blutro didn't laugh at Wolflock's jest. He looked sternly at the teenager with his stormy eyes.

"It was because your life was in danger. I have no means to discover why, but, several times, I saw signs that someone had tried to break into your room. It looked like they were trying to wedge a knife between the door and frame to jimmy it open. After what happened with Parihaan, the smuggling, the Tuiti fruit sickness and you being thrown overboard, I knew you were in danger, lad. Don't look so surprised," Captain Blutro scoffed, clapping his shoulder, and moving in closer so only Wolflock and Mothy could hear him. "I'm no fool to what goes in and on my ship."

Wolflock felt his face go numb, and it wasn't from the cold.

"I only hope that, now you are on shore, you're safe, but, to keep you uninjured, I am sending you both to the inn that me and all the crew stay at when we're here. The

Mermaid's Paddle. It's a good little inn, filled with rough folk like us, but no one dares start any nonsense, and nothing goes unnoticed by old Chosin. You'll be safe until you get on your way to Mystentine."

"I... why didn't you tell me sooner?" Wolflock frowned. Irritation grew in his throat as he realised the captain hadn't been taunting him with his ship duties like he was one of the crew, but he had been babying him.

"Because I knew full well you'd go looking for the culprit, and I couldn't be sure you'd come out of that altercation unscathed. I wasn't going to have you hurt, Wolflock. Don't look at me like that. Trust that your captain knew best."

Wolflock looked away, scowling. "It's not in my nature to give my autonomy over to any authority, Captain. Deserving or otherwise."

Captain Blutro sighed and clapped his shoulder. "And, for that, I am very pleased I made the decision I did. I may see you at the Mermaid's Paddle later today. Until then, try to stay out of trouble."

Wolflock groaned in exasperation. "Why is everyone telling me that? Don't they know that it's trouble that can't stay away from me?"

Rhiannon D. Elton

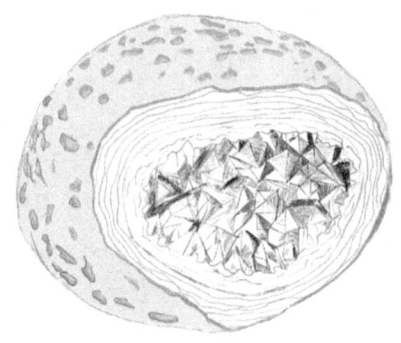

CHAPTER 3

Clear as Mud

Wolflock felt less inclined to say any more "merry part"s and turned into the marketplace along the bay's edge. Two long, crooked rows of market stalls splashed vibrant colours between the grey sky and the brown bay. Displays of hard baked cakes and candies, roasted nuts and local fruits sat on pinewood trays. Someone had intricately decorated each tray and set of shelves with burnt lines resembling ropes, knots, and interlocked patterns. Some had written along them in the jagged Shiriling script. Wolflock could see every stall had the exact same design with the same collapsible trestle table. Whoever was the carpenter for the town would have to be very well known. Between the clinking strings of shells, beads, clothing, and food, Wolflock's piercing eyes only needed to scan a few stalls once to find the maker's seal on the back post. Burnt into the pole with the same intertwined design, a set of two pine trees, one pointing up, the other pointing down, and an axe coming from the trunk that joined them. He spotted the same symbol on several other stalls and an empty table that had a note weighted by a stone on it reading:

Jergess the Cobbler is away due to illness. For all cobbling needs, book in at his house or send mail to Elli at Mystentine.

He wondered what a cobbler could be doing besides minor repairs and new laces at a market, but he couldn't see anything else in the rabble he would be interested in. While Wolflock moved through the bustling crowd, observing but not touching, Mothy groped and gawked at everything.

"Look at all the fish stuff!" he exclaimed, pointing to another fishbone trinket. "To work with such fine things, it must take so much skill."

"I think," Wolflock wrinkled his nose as a fresh

whiff of fish stew assaulted his nostrils, "that you'll find, as a doctor, that all of this is just monotonous repetition."

"Huh?" Mothy looked at him with a mouthful of seaweed jerky in his mouth.

"The more you do a fine motor task, the better you get at it."

"Fine motor?"

"Physical. Come now, Mothy! You're sharper than that."

"Oh, I know." He shrugged and offered another seaweed treat out to Wolflock, who politely raised his hand to reject it. "You just got so upset with the captain trying to look after you, I thought you needed a moment to feel clever."

"It has nothing to do with his care for my person. It is more to do with the fact that he didn't tell me. I thought he believed me to be at a level of competence and trustworthiness, and now it is evident that he did not."

They made it along the stone wall to the busy stall of children collecting rocks from the bay.

"What if he did it because he believed you were too capable? Like, he wanted to keep you safe and keeping you busy was all he knew how to do? Not everyone has your deductive abilities, Lockie. Some people have to go about things in a more ordinary fashion."

Wolflock hummed a noncommittal response, leaving Mothy's words to echo in the back of his mind as he watched a group of people walk away from the stall. Each of them held shattered rocks. Some rocks glittered with gemstones protruding out of them.

"For just a sentus, you could find a treasure!" shouted the tallest child. Wolflock raised an eyebrow. They couldn't be more than eleven or twelve.

"A treasure?" Mothy asked as he approached the table.

"That's right. You give us a sentus and choose a rock. We smash it in half, and you get to see what treasure you found!" The child grinned broadly, tucking a thick blonde lock under their grey hood.

"Umm... That one! I choose that one," Mothy pointed at the smoothest rock.

The child took it and passed it to a small boy who smashed a hammer down on it.

"Oh dear, sorry, sir. Just plain stone inside. Maybe next time."

"Interesting. And what treasures have come out of your stones today?" Wolflock asked, pinching his chin.

"Oh, all sorts, sir. Clear ones, red ones, purple ones. The favourite is the green ones, though. Malachite.

The folks in Mystentine love dissolving it into potions of all kinds."

"Do you have a trick for finding good stones?" Wolflock asked, picking up one and turning it over.

"We'd never give away the game, sir." The child tapped their nose with a cheeky grin. The other children snickered behind them.

Wolflock set the stone down and yawned. "Well, it's a simple game to win. I would say I could easily pick out your best stones and have the stall shut by lunchtime with a few good deimas in my pocket for it."

"Big talk, sir, for someone who hasn't even tried."

Wolflock laid both hands on the table and looked at the stones. Some were very lumpy, others had large craters in them. Some were smooth and pretty. He noticed that the smoother ones laid through the middle and the front. The lumpier they got, the closer to the back and sides they were.

"I choose this one," he said, picking up one that the stallholder had their own hands in front of.

With a scowl, the child flung the stone to the hammer child, and it cracked open, revealing a tiny cavern of amethyst crystals, perfectly lining the inside of the stone.

"Good work, sir. What luck." The child rolled

their eyes as others from behind them put another bucket on the wall's edge.

"It's not luck at all. The rocks with bubbles in them have formed differently, giving them their disfigured appearance. Those will be the ones hiding gemstones."

The child's face fell.

"Don't fret. Answer a few questions for me and I won't tell anyone around how to spoil your game. What's wrong with the water in the bay? It's it supposed to be the clearest in the land?"

The children avoided his eye for a few moments before one of the littlest children with dark brown hair piped up.

"Mam said not to go near it. Is bad."

"Yes. I can see that. But why?"

"The mayor said it's fine, but no one believes him. Mam said it was the miner's fault. They dug up some rock that poisoned the bay, and now no fish or plant can be gotten out of it. The water can't even be boiled for cooking or making brine with," said the ringleader.

"Yeah! Da said he can't make his famous fry fish with this water neither!"

The gaggle of children started squawking over the top of each other about how bad the water being brown had made the town. Wolflock raised his hands, and they fell quiet after a moment to finish their sentences.

"Why not just get what you need from a different part of the bay?"

The second tallest wiped their nose on their sleeve. "We did at first, but the brown has been seeping along all the pockets we used to go to. It's going along the shoreline right up until where the rivers meet the sea. It's too far for us to go every day."

"Too far? Why not take a carriage?"

"During the Pisces Moon? Fat chance," the ringleader scoffed.

"Why?" Mothy asked, as he paid for another rock to get smashed open.

"With everyone in Shiriling wanting to come in and out of the place, there is no way you can get a carriage to take you anywhere. During the festival, you basically have to stay put for a quarter moon or you walk. And we ain't walking halfway to Mystentine to get fish."

Wolflock's gut dropped. They'd wasted so much time.

"Mothy, let's go. We need to book our transport to Mystentine."

"But I wanted to go see a few more shops first. I have to pick up a hat for the trip. My hair is thinner than yours."

"If we don't go now, we may never be going at all!" Wolflock snapped. "Where's the nearest carriage depot?"

"To Mystentine? You want the North gate." The ringleader nodded, pointing up one of the broader roads. "Take the main road that way. You can't miss it."

Wolflock whirled about and took off at a run with Mothy in tow. Every moment running through this foreign town felt like an hour. He didn't think he'd be fighting against time again so soon. Every hiccup on the Silver Ice Hair had taken him hours, if not days, further from Mystentine. If he didn't make it up the top of the mountain by the first of Winter, the paths to the top would freeze over and he'd be stuck for at least three months, if not longer if the mountain didn't thaw in early Spring.

Three months...

Trapped with only a little money in a foreign city with no means to get by. He'd have to live in a temple or a boarding house where he'd have no freedom to do as he wished. He'd be better off working on the Silver Ice Hair until next year's intake!

He gritted his teeth and ran harder. His lungs burned against the cold air and the heat of his exertion running uphill against the chill made his stomach revolt.

He rounded a wide bend in the road and saw it. The North Gatehouse Stables. Only as he made it to the outskirts of the town did he realise that a giant wooden wall cupped the town against the bay. He didn't have time to marvel at the fan shell town design or the way the stone houses were built into a slope that looked both sturdy and cosy. His mind just focused on getting into the stable office.

He ran onto the wooden terrace and wrenched the door open. As he threw himself inside the stiflingly warm room, he collided with two tall figures that smelled of smoking herbs and medicine. One of them fell clean over, scattering jars of herbs all over the place.

"Out of the way!" Wolflock snapped and stumbled to the desk past them.

"Sorry, sir!" Mothy apologised as he tried to help the man up.

Wolflock threw himself at the counter.

Panting, lungs burning, he slammed his hand on the counter to the office and wheezed. "Two... to... Mystentine..."

The attendant, a young freckled burly lad, tilted his head to the side like a confused puppy.

"Two, two? So four?"

"No... Two to go... to Mystentine..." Wolflock

scowled.

"Tutu go to Mystentine? Who is Tutu? Are you a dance group?"

Wolflock wondered for a moment if the boy had an unnaturally thick skull. It heightened his instant dislike of the boy when his box-like jaw started chewing on some kind of gum.

"No. Now, listen." He inhaled slowly, catching his breath and summoning his Plughian authority to his voice. "The gentleman outside and I need to get a carriage to Mystentine. As soon as possible."

The boy still looked bewildered.

"Oh, aye? There ain't none left though for the week. Tha' gentleman just took the last one."

Wolflock turned his whole body to look back at Mothy between two men. A lean, grey jacketed Xiayahn looking man with almond-shaped eyes and a long black ponytail, and the familiar bald head of Stra. He sank to the floor as if someone had released plugs from his feet and let out all his enthusiasm.

"It's over... The cut-off date for new students is... we won't get there in time... it's over..." He could have cried, but all he could do was look dismally at the scuffed wooden floor.

He stared into the distance, not hearing the

perplexed counter boy try to speak to him. He barely heard the low chuckle of Stra as he approached.

"Merry meet again, Mr Felen," he smiled cheerfully and looked down at Wolflock. "I see you may be in need of a lift. You may be in luck."

Mothy, who had been talking to the man Wolflock had toppled into, stopped mid-sentence to listen.

"In luck?"

"Indeed," Stra continued speaking without reaching out to help Wolflock off the floor. "The last carriage was a four-seater. We may be a bit cramped, but it will still get you to Mystentine with just enough time to get up that mountain of yours."

"Really?" Wolflock slowly rose back onto his feet. "What would you like in return?"

His hazel eyes flashed, "Oh, nothing. To be honest, I am looking forward to having company on the journey. It will be a long and boring one without it. If you must, think of it as thanks for making those pesky fortune tellers depart sooner than later. They were quite the bother."

Wolflock felt like Stra wasn't being entirely honest, but he didn't care. The man could ask for payment later. Maybe it was solving some private puzzle or finding a lost item. Whatever it was, it simply relieved Wolflock they had the transport they needed.

"Thank you, Stra. Thank you so very much. I am exceedingly grateful."

"A young man's higher education is imperative to his future. Our carriage leaves tomorrow just after breakfast. I'll come and collect you. Where were you and Mr Enitnelav staying?"

"At the Mermaid's Paddle. We haven't been there just yet but, hopefully, the captain delivered our luggage there."

"Lovely! I'll see you then. Sorry to cut this short, Mr Felen, but I must be off. I have business here before we leave tomorrow. Merry part."

Wolflock reached out with his left hand automatically, catching Stra by surprise. The thin, bald man swapped two little red tickets from one hand to the other. The hole punched edge he glimpsed said something about cargo and two tonnes. It had the same brand mark on it as the stalls and tables in the market; the two pines and axe.

His long, yellowed fingers gripped Wolflock's like a falcon's claws and, with a single shake, he nodded and departed. He wondered, for a moment, why Stra was ordering a cargo trailer as well as a carriage. He didn't seem to have that much stock on the ship. Perhaps he purchased more or had something waiting for him. He wasn't left too long to ponder as Mothy bounced up to Wolflock's side, shoving his shoulder with excitement.

"See? It all worked out! No need to worry like you do."

"The only thing I'm worried about now is being too cramped in the carriage."

Rhiannon D. Elton

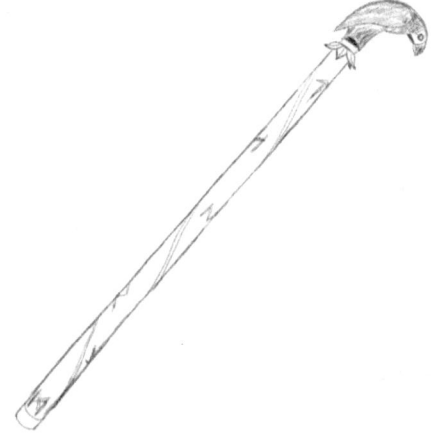

CHAPTER 4

The Doctor of Many Pockets

Wolflock felt as if he could breathe and, as the light of the frosty sun pierced the clouds, his mood lifted. With their business concluded, he nodded curtly to the dumbfounded attendant before stepping outside with Mothy at his heels.

"Lockie, you have to meet Dr Qwan. He's travelled all over and is a resident in town. He's said he'll be our guide to Creast."

Wolflock nodded politely to Dr Qwan, not yet reaching out his hand to shake in case he'd offended the man after knocking him over moments before. He wanted to gauge the manners of this stranger, as well as still feeling a little irritated that the doctor had gotten in the way in his first place.

"Merry meet, doctor. That's very kind of you to offer to show us around. You may address me as Mr Wolflock Felen."

"Pfft. An absolute pleasure to make your acquaintance, Mr Wolflock Felen. Just call me Dr Qwan. Everyone does. Or Qwan if it suits you." He spoke quickly with a lopsided smile. Wolflock didn't like the way he enunciated his full name. It felt like the doctor was making fun of him. "Showing people around is not a problem at all," the doctor continued. "This sleepy little town gets so boring. The arrival of your ship's company coinciding with the Pisces Moon festival is the most fun I've had all year. Except for the goat pox plague last Spring. That was riveting."

"Goat pox?" Mothy asked with well-timed curiosity.

"Oh yes. Not common this far West, but, boy, oh boy, did it hit us hard. Residents climbing vertical walls and chewing cardboard everywhere."

Wolflock saw a hint of a smirk on Dr Qwan's sharp face, and he realised his 'goat pox' story was a joke for tourists. He didn't bother retaining any information past that point in the conversation, but, instead, took a moment to analyse Dr Qwan's attire and features. From the shape of his dark brown almond eyes, he had Xiayahn heritage, but his skin was tanned with a rich golden hue, unlike Nu's family's porcelain skin, only kissed with colour from their travels.

Dr Qwan's long black hair whipped in a sleek ponytail when he turned his head. His movements were so exaggerated and his speech patterns so varied that it was hard to sift the truth from falsehoods. Not because his mannerisms were masterful, but, rather, everything he said to Mothy was a fantastical lie. Or at the minimum, a very exaggerated truth.

"Shall we make our way to breakfast? I'm famished after our morning's exercise," Wolflock cut in, sensing that Dr Qwan could speak for hours without pause if he had as captive an audience as Mothy.

"You mean lunch, Mr Wolflock Felen." Dr Qwan waggled his finger as they set off.

"No," Wolflock sniffed. "I mean breakfast. We are yet to have our first meal of the day."

"I mean... I'd be happy with breakfast and lunch

about now." Mothy's shoulders rose around his ears as his stomach agreed loudly.

Wolflock rolled his eyes. "Honestly, Mothy, if you ever went twelve hours without food you'd evaporate."

"Don't know what that means. Where is good for a breakfast lunch combination, Dr Qwan?"

"Ah," Qwan said with a wise tone, "this is why I said it was lunchtime. There is only one place in Creast that knows how to use breakfast leftovers to create lunch masterpieces. Follow me, boys."

Wolflock eyed the doctor as they marched down a main road. He could tell the doctor was an eccentric and intelligent man who was quite well off by his coat. A long-sleeved soft leather white coat that reached his wrists and the backs of his knees. The leather was exceptionally well kept, but, after the initial purchase, someone had sewn all manner of pockets to the inside and out of the coat. He also had various traces of strange colours splashed over his cuff. It appeared to be a swirling rainbow of water colour accidents, but Wolflock could smell the odd metallic traces of experiments.

He could see pinches of herbs clinging to the corners of his pockets, seashells bulging in others, and he could have sworn he saw something wriggle in his deep side pocket. The only jewellery he wore was a knotted band around his left ring finger. His laugh was contagious and many people throughout the town waved to him as they put up various decorations for the festival.

Wolflock had taken little notice as they had made their run to the North Gate Cart Services, but the town was being adorned in blue paper lanterns and wreaths of evergreens. The townspeople made most of them of pine, but some wreaths looked like a blend of oak, cedar and ivy all woven together. The earthy smell mixed with the pungent aroma of tree sap made the entire town smell of Spring, even though they were only a half moon from Winter.

"... And that's how I knew it was just wind and not a baby."

Mothy belly laughed at the doctor's joke.

"Is this all for the Pisces Moon festival?" Wolflock asked as he noted thin metal and ceramic fish decorations being strung all along the streets, zigzagging all the way to the wharves. The stone and wooden buildings glittered with the decorative fish in the mid-morning sun.

"That it is, Mr Wolflock Felen," Dr Qwan stopped his story for a moment to answer with a kind smile.

"So, what do you normally treat here in town?" Mothy asked, as he wiped tears of laughter from his eyes.

"Oh, you know... Colds, flus, sometimes I teach

people how to resuscitate the drowned. Mostly I treat poisons from the sea creatures and Small-Town-Itis for people who have moved to Creast from Mystentine," Qwan shrugged.

"Small-town-itis?"

"Oh, aye. Mystentine is the largest city in the North. I'd say it rivals Corl for population size, but everything is much closer together. So people come here thinking they want to escape from the hustle and bustle of the big city, only to find that they can't relax in this little town. The hilarity of it is what I live for."

"You'll have to show me how to resuscitate a drowned person!" Mothy's eyes sparkled blue with delight.

"I'd like to hear more about your antidotes," Wolflock hummed, watching as a girl received a reprimand for a fallen streamer. She'd been ogling them as they strode past and dropped the streamer, allowing several paper lanterns to bend to the will of gravity. "Why is the Pisces Moon such a big festival in these parts?"

"Well, Mr Wolflock Felen, the people here live a fairly barren lifestyle. It's hard to farm much in the cold and so they rely on fish throughout the year, but fresh fish doesn't last long. When the water freezes, the fish migrate down the river and then return in mid-Spring. So, to survive, we dry it. Dried fish isn't all that appetising. Once a year on the night of the Pisces Moon, all the mermaids in the sea come to the shore. They drive thousands of fishes out right into our hands and we're able to last through the Winter safely. They also bring out all kinds of seaweeds and sea fruits that we can use as well. If anyone doesn't know what the mermaids have brought out, they give it to me, and I see if it has medicinal properties."

His wicked smirk told Wolflock that he may play pranks on the townsfolk with his knowledge.

"Why here though? Creast isn't the only town along the sea. Is it because it is the biggest?" Mothy asked.

"In the bay there is a giant jewel. When the moonlight is just right, it shines down onto the jewel and the mermaids perform their courtship ritual around it. It must be very special to them. Here we are! Shackled Sheckle's Shocked Speckled Hen."

The boys both blinked at the name and then snickered.

"Please tell me there is a story behind that." Mothy stifled his laughter as best he could.

"I'll let Sheckle tell you himself. They do the best roast chicken I've ever tasted in my life, though."

The wide townhouse building nestled against a

larger multi-storeyed municipal office and was far more welcoming with the enticing scent of baking herbs and chicken wafting onto the street. Roasted potatoes, pumpkin and other root vegetables cooked away in their minds as Dr Qwan led them inside.

The clink of cutlery on clay plates and the chatter of a busy establishment met their ears. Wolflock heard the scrap of a poker against burning logs and saw a tall man in an apron close the grate over the open fireplace. As he looked around at the other patrons chatting, he noted many of them had cardboard folders and leather cases on their tables or beside their chairs. He noted they all wore high leather boots, tight trousers and different length waistcoats with contrasting hems and large shiny buttons. It seemed to be a sort of unofficial uniform amongst them. Although the restaurant had a homely, welcoming presence, it was also clearly a favourite place for town officials to conduct business in comfort.

"Now, not just any table will do for my esteemed guests. Sheckle! Your best table please." Dr Qwan waved to the man with the apron.

"Now, now, Qwan," Sheckle raised his hands as if to settle Dr Qwan's high spirits pre-emptively, "The mayor has the booth at the-"

"Excellent! He's expecting me. I'll see us through,

my good man. Later, you have to tell these lads about the shackled speckled hen as well."

Qwan stepped over a thick red rope cordoning off the stairs. Mothy followed him with a coy smile, but Wolflock continued analysing everything down his indifferent nose. A few of the officials looked up, but no one stopped the doctor, so Wolflock deemed it safe to proceed after him.

At the top of the stairs, Dr Qwan unclipped another thick rope and bowed to the boys as they passed through. They came to a large wooden landing that overlooked most of the seating area below. A thick green carpet covered wooden floors and an intricately carved partition gave privacy to the people seated around the table. Wolflock and Mothy both jumped as someone slammed their hands violently onto the wood.

"You can't be serious!" roared a gravely man's voice. "If my Guard spends all day carting water back and forth, how am I meant to find the source of this mess?"

"Jaimeron, please," came a simpering plea. "We're under enough strain as it is. Let's get through this evening and we'll go from there. It's not a hard task, is it? You're the only one I can trust with it."

"Just get her to shut her blasted mine! That's where it's coming from!" another man yelled.

"You say that one more time and I'll shut you in it." The coldness of the woman's voice who spoke gave Wolflock a chill. He'd heard something like that low tone before when he'd seen a wild dog attacking a foal. Starving and desperate to feed her pups in the middle of Winter, even cornered by three grooms folk, she had summoned more will than most humans he knew. "Since you've shut off the river through town, it should be you who has to answer for this disease."

"It wasn't me! It was the gods who froze the river early because of your damn digging!"

Wolflock heard a chair scrape on the floor as someone stood up rapidly.

"Liar! You're a filthy liar! Ack!"

The woman coughed and other people in the room moved, likely to aid her.

"Now, now, now," eased a man with a voice like crushed velvet. "We all want to know where the murk in the water came from, but, right now, it's more important to make sure the townspeople are all happy and healthy. You've sent for aid from Mystentine, I presume, Mayor Herfed? As we spoke about last Lucimpus in my office?"

"Y-yes, yes. Of course! They will definitely be here in due time," came the stammer of the simpering man with a voice filled with cheeks.

"Then, as long as we have a few people assisting over the course of the festival, it will be business as usual! I will personally inspect the mine for any issues. That frees up Jaimeron's guard and puts a pin in this infection business. And, before you raise any objections, Vanmoinen, the relationship between my son and Jaxarna's daughter will not impede my judgement in the slightest. Does that sound fair?" the velvety voice asked.

"Oh, Mr Mayor Herfed Merlai," sang Dr Qwan, ignoring the conversation Wolflock was becoming quite fascinated with.

The room fell silent as Dr Qwan thrust the partition open with a grand sweeping gesture. "May I humbly present: Mothy, and the esteemed Mr Wolflock Felen!"

Wolflock glared at the doctor as Mothy took a deep bow.

"Loong? What are you doing here?" The mayor hiccupped, wiping his ginger beard with a napkin. "I had this booth booked, you know?"

"Oh? You know Sheckle. He's not about to stop me from having the best seat in the house. Nice to see you all." He gestured to the five people around the table. "Mothy, Mr Wolflock Felen, please meet: Mayor Herfed Merlai, Jaimeron the leader of our local guard, Jaxarna our brickmaker and mineral finder, Vanmoinen our lumberjack and carpenter, and, of course, the noble Lord Therym."

Wolflock's eyes looked over all of them on the dim landing. The way they were all skulking here reminded him of the drama his nemesis back in Plugh would get into. Talking behind a screen in a dark room was something Wolflock expected Plughian politicians to do. The darkness didn't lend itself to his inquisitive eyes, either.

"My, my, my," Dr Qwan tutted, squeezing himself between the brickmaker and the nobleman to turn the dial on the oil lamp in the middle of the table. "If it were any darker in here, we'd be playing blind man's bluff. That's better. Oh! Jaxarna. I see you've been working hard today."

The doctor snickered as he brushed flakes of dried orange clay from his white coat. As the light grew, Wolflock could see that the hard-faced woman was covered from head to toe in crusty flakes. He could see everywhere her hands had been on her chair and table from it and when she moved, it cracked along her tight scalp braids, revealing threads of silver in her ash brown hair.

Jaxarna grunted at the doctor, her eyes fixed in a

deadly stare at the short, spiky-bearded man across the table. Three wooden rings clasped the trio of braids in his short golden-brown beard and Wolflock noted his calloused fingers poking out of his bandaged hands and the flecks of sawdust caught in his wiry arm hairs.

Ah, the carpenter, he surmised.

"Let me get you all a seat." The mayor swallowed, his blue eyes darting to the faces of the current committee around the table. When none of them made eye contact with him, he froze as if he needed permission they weren't giving.

The tallest of the lot stood up with both hands clenched into fists on the table. "Don't bother. I'll speak to you when you aren't 'entertaining'."

"J-Jaimeron-" the mayor stammered and tried to squeeze out around the chairs of the nobleman and the bricklayer.

The bricklayer, Jaxarna, blocked him off, rising and walking away without another word.

"Now, now." The man called Therym patted the mayor's arm until he sat back down, looking out after the leaving parties. "I'm sure after an hour they'll be fine. Don't fret. It's more important for you to be the face of the festival. No one else is getting sick?"

The way the man lowered his tone and stroked the

mayor's arm, which made Wolflock's hairs on the back of his neck prickle. It looked uncannily like what the Thorn family would do back in Plugh to manipulate the local politicians.

"No. No. I mean; a few people have coughs and colds but nothing serious."

Wolflock watched the mayor sweat, and his voice held no confidence. He couldn't help but think that every single person around that table had been lying to each other.

"Is there anything I can do to help the sick?" Dr Qwan asked as he pulled a few platters of uneaten dried fruits, nuts, and salted meats to himself. Mothy began doing the same, piling an unused plate in front of himself. Wolflock observed the interaction as he took a seat on the far side of the table next to Mothy.

"I suppose I'll head off too. I wanted to say before I left, though," the carpenter stood and tucked his chair in, "you would do well to investigate that mine thoroughly. It's dangerous and I'm sure you'll find the source of everything going wrong there. I trust you to do it without preference." The carpenter Vanmoinen spoke to Therym as if he were in charge, only glancing at the mayor.

The mayor nodded and gave a weak smile. "I will

look into it for you, Vanmoinen. Now, make sure we have enough wood for the cooper. I'm sure we'll have a tremendous batch of fish this evening."

Vanmoinen the carpenter left and Wolflock watched the mayor's demeanour completely collapse for a few moments when he was out of sight.

"Sorry, terribly sorry. What were your names again?"

"This is Mothy, the travelling medical enthusiast, and Mr Wolflock Felen, Mr Mayor Herfed Merlai." Dr Qwan waved his hands theatrically, sending a few almonds pinging across the room.

"Ah. I take it you introduced yourself much the same as I did. A tragic curse to show any pomp to Dr Qwan, I must say. He'll make fun of you for that until he dies. Perhaps even longer." The barrel-chested mayor chuckled, but not from his belly.

"I have always said that laughter is the best medicine. Besides actual medicine, of course. What seemed to be the problem with our esteemed tradesfolk?"

"It's-"

"Oh, it's nothing to be troubled about," Therym the noble cut the mayor off. "There's been a large blame game about the murk in the bay and the little flu that's popped up. Nothing for anyone to worry about."

Wolflock's irritation as the man dismissed all the surrounding concerns grew beyond what his propriety could hold back.

"But surely a doctor would be able to analyse the water contents and see if it is in fact infected with something that may impact the town. How long has this been going on for? And I heard the carpenter has shut off a river to the bay. Would that impact the town in any significant capacity?"

The nobleman blinked, taken aback, but his saccharine smile quickly resumed, and he stared directly into Wolflock's eyes. "Your accent? From Plugh, I suspect. I have business in Plugh. Did you say your surname was Felen? Excellent family. Best horses in all of Puinteyle, dare I say."

Wolflock felt the compliment as a slug trying to find a crack in the window of a kitchen. The slimy politics of 'nobility' never failed to bring out his most petulant side.

"Surely a doctor could test the water to see what kind of sickness is affecting the townsfolk. The children on the docks said that even boiling the water from the bay won't make it usable for brine. That doesn't sound like everything is fine."

The mayor paled, his beady blue eyes darting

around for an escape. Therym's dark brown eyes narrowed as he looked down his nose at Wolflock. He leaned forward, clinking his thick golden chains over his fox fur overcoat. He was significantly older than anyone else in the room and this seemed to carry gravity on everyone except Wolflock. Even Dr Qwan stopped fidgeting.

"What are you, Mr Wolflock Felen?" he whispered loud enough for everyone to hear.

Wolflock's mouth twitched uncomfortably. He understood the question, but he didn't have an answer. He wasn't yet a student, nor was he employed. It felt repugnant to use his title, as it held little weight outside of Plugh, but he also didn't want to use the distasteful term in front of Mothy. He couldn't say he was a sailor or a traveller without losing power in the situation.

He opened his mouth to stall.

"He's the best appraising investigator in all the North Zilber River," Mothy chirped after swallowing a large mouthful.

"Yes. Yes, that's right. Thank you, Mothy," Wolflock said as he looked at his friend with immense relief.

"Appraising what?" Mayor Merlai asked.

"Sounds like some sort of artefact finder or an

auctioneer," Therym leaned over to the mayor to loudly whisper again.

"Definitely not," Wolflock cut in. "I solve problems. I appraise if they're worth my time and I get to the truth of the matter. Several people required my assistance during my stay on the Silver Ice Hair. Finding lost pets, children, and helping unveil incidents aboard the ship for insurance purposes." It felt so odd coming from his own lips.

"He also found the source of a terrible sickness. I, myself, would have died if he hadn't stopped the illness. We definitely wouldn't have made it to Creast on time."

"You're very right, Mothy. Thank you again. We would not have made it here with the extra rations of fish from Irid before the festival."

"Extra rations? You're mistaken, Mr Felen. We send our fish to Irid. Not the other way around." Therym's large grey eyebrows pinched.

Before Wolflock could argue, the mayor rang the bell rope behind him, and Sheckle trotted up to the landing. "More food, sir?"

"Not for me, Sheckle. Please bring Dr Qwan's favourite. I owe him for his assistance with the goat plague. Has he told you the story?"

"Not one I would have believed," Wolflock

snorted and leaned back in his chair, arms folded.

"Well! Allow me to regale you with one of Dr Qwan's most incredible feats. Around six weeks ago we had a strange cargo ship pass through. It transported lots of goat meat, but I believe it had all gone bad. Before I could inquire about it, they had shot through town, but not before selling it all to the townspeople. Remember, Therym? They had those ornate eye logos on their butcher paper."

"Yes. Very unique. If you don't mind, Herfed, I'll head off now. I must get things ready for the festival this evening." Therym nodded and picked up his elegant black cane with a handle shaped like a silver eagle. Wolflock saw how he ran his forefinger over the worn head in a habitual manner. He smiled at everyone as he left, but he made the least eye contact with Wolflock.

"Very well. I'll see you this evening. As I was saying, the meat was rotten and most of the town grew terribly ill."

"What was wrong with them?" Mothy asked, looking between the mayor and the doctor.

"A kind of dysentery. I thought at first it was food poisoning, but the specific illness was highly contagious. There must have been illness in the food. All I did was make sure everyone had at least four pints of river water a day and plenty of fish soup," Dr Qwan yawned.

"It was like magic that he wiped out the goat plague in just a few days. Any longer and we would have had to chip into our winter stores."

"Oh, Mr Mayor Herfed Merlai! Stop! You're making me blush."

"But you used an algae too! Remember? To clean the water!" Mayor Merlai prompted.

"Ah yes." Dr Qwan's bored face grew into a more genuine smile as he looked at Wolflock and Mothy to explain. "There is an algae that grows in the streams just outside the town. It glows in the dark so you can't miss it at night. It consumes filth and purifies it. Only works in freshwater, though. I tried using it in the bay. I think it loves pine oils, to be honest. It always glows stronger near the lumbermill. Lucky the merfolk will be here tonight though, eh?"

"Huh? Oh! Oh yes. Very lucky indeed..." Mayor Merlai's tone shrank.

"Why is it lucky?" Wolflock rolled a half-shelled walnut in his fingers.

"Well," Dr Qwan bent his index finger under his chin thoughtfully, "they'll drive the fish from the bay for us to collect for Winter before the water can infect them. The colder it gets, the fewer fish we find in the rivers and meat from the forests."

"I'm sure it will be perfectly fine. We'll ask Mystentine to give us anything extra if a few fish aren't right."

"But what about the mermaids?" Wolflock frowned, thinking of Himi and how her family might be affected by the toxic water.

"My good lad, they will be fine. They're much bigger than fish. Much stronger, too. Enjoy your meal, Dr Qwan. I have to speak with the temple before everything happens tonight, so I'll see you all later. Merry part."

Wolflock jumped to his feet and slammed his hands on the table, shaking the plates. "But what about clearing the bay? You're just going to let it rot and kill mermaids as well as your people?"

"Excuse me?" Mayor Merlai huffed, astounded at the accusation. "You don't know anything-"

"I know what a politician looks like when he's been bought. Just tell me why you want to kill off your entire town for money?"

"Y-you've got it all wrong-"

Wolflock narrowed his eyes. "You're right. It's not money. It's prestige. Your prestige. You landed a career as a politician in an affluent town with a huge festival that brings people for miles. You have the best craftsfolk and doctors outside of Mystentine, and they function at minimal costs. The only thing you have to do is to be honey between cakes and, with the first issue you're being called on to solve for the sake of your people's lives, you baulk. How is everyone going to feel when they find out you haven't asked for assistance from the capital city because you didn't want to affect tourism? And, judging by the amount of fish you ordered in reserve from Irid, you only have three weeks before your people starve. And, for what? The economy? Politicians like you make me sick."

Mayor Merlai puffed up with indignation, pointing his thick finger at Wolflock's hooked nose. "Now see here-"

"That's nothing new, Mr Appraising Investigator," Dr Qwan chuckled from his seat. "We've all known that for weeks now."

CHAPTER 5

The Mine is Greener
on the Other Side

Wolflock watched the mayor go through a tremendous transformation. He deflated, went red-faced, tried to raise his hand in authority, and finally paled and slumped back into his seat.

"I had no idea. I am so sorry. I am just so sorry. I've had so many people from the docks ask me to investigate the murk in the bay. They all think it's the mine that Jaxarna just bought. She's barely begun her excavations, and this is already happening. Then the river stopped flowing a season early and I'm up for an award if the university folk coming to study the mermaid phenomenon find anything worthwhile. We've never had to ask for assistance to feed ourselves during the Winter since the gemstone was first given to the bay. I am going to look like such a fool. I could have acted all this time. I thought I was saving face!"

Dr Qwan looked at both Wolflock and Mothy before shrugging. "No one actually knows. Thanks for coming clean, though. Doesn't that feel better?"

Wolflock grinned, impressed with Dr Qwan's bluff. Mayor Merlai looked as if someone had hit him over the head with a wet fish.

"I... You... I beg your pardon?"

"These boys here are quite bright. Brightest ones I've seen today. And, for your benefit, they're eager to help solve this problem. With my help, they just might be able to. Wouldn't this all be better if it were actually solved, and the bay was clean again? No more murk, and Creast is back to its full glory."

"But how could it possibly be solved?" Mayor Merlai pleaded.

"Didn't you hear Mothy earlier? You have the best apparatus investor in all the North of the Zilber River!"

"Appraising investigator," Wolflock corrected.

"That too. We need to know what you know, though. Tell us whatever you think will help."

Wolflock shoved himself directly across the table from the mayor, "Spare no details at all."

Mayor Merlai exhaled, letting his shoulders drop in surrender. "I don't want to admit it, but I think the source is from Jaxarna's mine. It is in a cave system right on the edge of the bay. It was only a day or so after she began her work in there that this all began. She used the last of her savings to purchase the copper mine. Once dug out, she wanted to transform it into an underwater viewing area with glass panels. If she took donations for entry, she believed she could live comfortably for the rest of her days. She's not well, so the rest of her days might be sooner than later. And she's been thinking about her daughter, clearly. Wanting to set up a light form of work to help her."

"Her daughter's name is Girid," Dr Qwan informed Mothy and Wolflock. "Pretty girl who's much more slight than her mother. Not built up from hard labour. Engaged to Lord Therym's son."

"I didn't want to stop her progress, but it's been two weeks, and this is only getting worse. I'm worried about her health and the health of the town."

"And your reputation," Wolflock snipped.

"When that is all you have skill to build, then that is all you can be concerned about, boy," Mayor Merlai retorted with more spine than Wolflock had seen from him.

"I suppose we'll go and check this mine first and question Jaxarna. Dr Qwan, would you be confident in discovering a contagion leaking from the mine?"

"Let me check..." the doctor mumbled as he felt through his pockets. He placed his hand in a deep back pocket, revealing a bottle of powder and a scratched Petrie dish. "Ahah! Yes. Yes, this should be fine. As long as it's water born, we'll know if it matches the bay."

The mayor looked amazed at the experiment, but Wolflock pulled Mothy to his feet. Keen to get moving, Wolflock ushered Mothy and Dr Qwan away without allowing Mayor Merlai to ask how the doctor's chemistry worked.

Dr Qwan led them through town and around the Northern part of the bay towards a grassy path that took them to the mines. As they walked through town, Wolflock took more notice of the health of the people. They were mostly pale because of the decreased sunlight, even the people with darker skin had a translucent look to them. The people moved in a slow, tired fashion. Wolflock knew that, in Plugh, festivals meant everyone would rush around with a mixture of excitement and nervousness that he himself found grating. The lack of enthusiasm was unsettling.

The sea breeze and light stroll gave Wolflock enough calm to think about the information he had and the data he still needed.

The infection in the bay had made the townsfolk sick. It was a saltwater bay and, on the night of the Pisces Moon festival, the mermaids would come to the bay for their courtship rituals. Two weeks ago, the brickmaker, Jaxarna, who is known to be unwell, purchased a mine with all her savings. Her daughter was presently engaged to the nobleman Therym's son. Around that same time, the river that ran through town from the lumber mill to the bay stopped flowing. The carpenter Vanmoinen said it was frozen over because of the gods being displeased. Vanmoinen blamed Jaxarna for the bay's infection and she blamed him right back.

Wolflock would not believe either of their words without actual, conclusive proof.

"Well, this is as far as we're allowed to go." Dr Qwan stopped, making Wolflock bump into Mothy's back absentmindedly.

"Huh? Why?" he frowned.

"Well, one of the reasons Jaxarna got this place so

cheap was because it's haunted?"

"Haunted? Honestly?" Wolflock sighed through his nose and crossed his arms. Mothy looked nervous.

"Oh, yes. Yes, indeed. Very haunted. The most haunted of anywhere in town. Except the old cave by the forest."

"And what do you normally do about ghosts in town?"

"Smoke them out. A good old seining with some mugwort and rosemary does the trick, but the kids do that here all the time and she still comes back. Legend says she's a widow who died trying to sing her husband back home from a ruinous voyage."

"Back at home you had to appease them to get rid of them," Mothy piped up. "That's the tricky bit though. I remember one time one of the ghosts wanted a slice of pie but everyone thought it had something to do with a lost necklace. Months of lost forks."

"Have you got any records of such a case in the town library?"

Dr Qwan shrugged with his sheepish grin. Wolflock huffed and walked past the doctor into the ramshackle entrance to the mine. Someone had hobbled together the braces of wood haphazardly, but the wood was pale enough to indicate it hadn't been cut all that long ago.

The carpenter and brick maker have only fallen out recently. He cut the wood and sold it to her, Wolflock thought as he ran his hand along the smooth beam. But he wouldn't put it together for her, probably because he was mad. But what about? The mine? The sickness in the bay? Or something else...

The enchanting song of a woman interrupted his thoughts within the caves. The echoing tune wove around them like the most pristine orchestral notes.

"See? Siren. Told you."

"Doubtful. I am pleased by the music, but I'm not charmed," Wolflock snorted and entered the dark tunnel.

As he walked on, he felt Dr Qwan tug at his ear, pulling him closer to inspect him.

"Ay!"

"Ah, yes. Well, I suppose that's just it, isn't it?" the doctor mumbled absentmindedly as Mothy snorted back laughter.

Wolflock slapped his hands away, stumbling incredulously into the stony wall, "What's 'it'?"

"Well, I can hear her more clearly, as I have healthier ears than you. It's a testament to my longevity, you see. Incredibly healthy ears are a sign of good kidneys."

Wolflock scowled, pushing off the wall to stand up straight again. He couldn't help but notice the texture of the wall. It was bubbly, just like the children's geodes at the docks. He also noticed that his thumb ran along a strange scratch in the stone, smoothing out a portion of the stone in a short, thick line.

"Mothy, come see." He waved his hand at his friend. "Have you got a light? I want to make out what this strange mark is."

Mothy patted himself down and shook his head. A sizzle and flash of light emanated from the doctor as he lit a strange looking white match. It looked like a bone and burned with a bright white flame.

"Huh. I thought this was only useful for night time surgeries and mouths."

"What is that?" Wolflock asked, frustrated that he was so curious about the strange doctor's item. The match wasn't burning down.

"It's a ghost match. Said to be made of a bone from the wizard Antrum's hand after they died when both the sun and moon sat in the sky. Never burns out and the flame can't catch on anything. Look, it even burns cold. You can put your hair in it, and it won't even sizzle."

Wolflock's eyes widened with wonder. What a

useful and fantastical item. Dr Qwan chuckled at his expression and held the little match to the wall for them.

Someone had indeed carved away the stone in a line as thick as a finger and just as long. It scratched the charcoal rock to an off white with traces of a silvery metal.

"Iron wouldn't do this... I don't think steel would either," Wolflock said, more to himself than the others. As he examined the scratch on the wall, he saw that they had made several other marks along the wall at different heights. The strange markings sometimes went as deep as to reveal a greenish rock beneath, and others cut through to seams of copper. "She definitely purchased a wealthy mine. These must be her testing cuts. Why are no operations set up in here yet?"

Dr Qwan and Mothy looked at each other as Wolflock continued speaking to himself. The singing stopped as a loud, barking cough echoed through the hallway. The three of them made their way down the dark tunnel with a hasty step, seeing lights flickering towards the end.

Wolflock was the first to step into the well-lit auditorium at the end of the tunnel. In the centre of the large room was a large, deep pond that shone with a forest green hue from the stones in it. A hole in the ceiling let in a glittering beam of pale sunlight, and torches around the edge of the cavern lit passageways to other areas of the mine.

Along the edge of the pond was Jaxarna bent over, coughing, and a young, slender woman with earthy brown hair rubbing her back. Their faces looked so similar that Wolflock thought it was a safe guess that this was Girid, her daughter.

Dr Qwan trotted ahead of them, rifling through his pockets for a small bottle. "Here." He held the vial of clear, strong-smelling liquid under her nose. She gave two more coughs before they ceased immediately. Jaxarna cleared her throat as if she was going to cough again, but she kept the bottle under her nose, suppressing it.

"Doc... What are you doing here?"

"Trespassing," Dr Qwan shrugged.

Girid laughed a high, tinkling laugh. Wolflock expected Jaxarna to be angry, but she smiled with relief.

"I brought friends I could outrun in case you still felt upset."

Again, the women laughed. Jaxarna coughed again before putting the bottle under her nose once more.

"As your doctor, I'm going to have to insist you stop any sort of happiness or humour. Laughing is apparently killing you."

Jaxarna's face went red as she tried to hold back

another laugh, taking deep, slow breaths into her rattling chest. Wolflock and Mothy moved forward, taking in the cave's beauty. The pool in the middle had a natural stone bridge leading to its centre, and Wolflock thought it looked like a stadium for mermaids as the rocks around him stepped down in a funnel towards the centre. He could hear the sounds of lapping waves from a tunnel heading down towards the bay. The odd green pool could cause the contamination in the bay, but what would make it turn brown?

"Does the water from the bay ever reach this cavern?" he asked.

Jaxarna put her hand on her thick chest and took another deep breath of Dr Qwan's bottle. "No. No, never. Not even high tide. This all comes from rain and snow water."

"Does it ever overflow and spill into the bay?"

Jaxarna's eyes narrowed as she guessed his meaning. "No. It dries out plenty enough to let more water flow into it without overflowing. Qwan, what's your friend's questions about?"

"Not sure, but as the world's best up roaring instigator, I trust his judgement."

"Appraising investigator," Wolflock corrected. "And, thank you. What is in your mine?"

"Copper."

"Anything else?"

"Not tha' I'm aware of."

"Interesting..."

"Did Vanmoinen send you down here?" she snarled. "Because, if he did, you can tell that sap sucking son of a-"

"I can assure, ma'am, he did not. I'm here because if the water in the bay is harmful to mermaids, then a good friend of mine may be in mortal danger."

She scrutinised his face long and hard, then finally conceded with another cough. "It's... ack... just copper. As far as I know, at least. We might find a diamond or two," she wheezed, a laugh at Girid, who returned a sad smile.

"Let's get you into the fresh air." Dr Qwan ushered Jaxarna towards the entrance.

"It's faster out the back way. C'mon Qwan," she said as she led him through the Northeast tunnel.

Girid, Wolflock and Mothy stayed behind in the auditorium. Mothy skimmed a few stones and sang in a mock opera fashion, making Girid smile. From her tense, closed posture, her head dipped down and her shy eyes, Wolflock suspected it would be easy for her to clam up, but she seemed attentive to her mother. Perhaps she had information they could use. He saw her giggle at Mothy and had a stroke of inspiration. With no one seeing, Wolflock practised stretching his face into a wide grin like Mothy did and bounced on the balls of his feet a bit to generate the same bubbly energy.

"Can you shatter glass? We heard your singing earlier," he chimed in a voice much higher than his normal tone.

Mothy stopped dead, eyeing him carefully.

"Oh?" Girid giggled, looking at him with a bashful smile. "I... I haven't tried."

"It was so beautiful. I bet it makes your ma happy to hear it. Do you often sing for her while she works?"

Mothy continued to stare as if someone had wrung out his brain.

"She loves it. Mama's always encouraged my singing. She works so hard, so I don't have to labour. She always said as long as she could, she would support me. The least I can do is sing for her."

"That is so sweet. I wish my sister thought the same way," Wolflock sighed heavily, dropping his shoulders in exaggerated lamenting. "How long has she had that cough for? You must be worried."

"Oh... She just works too hard," Girid raised her shoulders, wrapping her arms around herself.

Wolflock could sense he was losing her stream of information as she closed off, so when she turned her face away from him, he waved wildly at Mothy to help him, only to quickly resume his original posture when she looked back. "Do you think it's from working in the mine?"

"Maybe..."

"I'm conducting a bit of training with Dr Qwan." Mothy cleared his throat and stepped forward, walking stiffly. "You seem to be a well-informed young lady. Perhaps you've seen something in this mine or your mother that she is unaware of?"

Wolflock gave Mothy a look to say, "not what I meant but, very well" before turning back to Girid, "Parents often push through even when it isn't good for them. All for the sake of their kids. Maybe apprentice Dr Enitnelav can help put some pieces together."

"Well..." Girid bit her lip and clutched her upper arms, "She's always been prone to chest conditions. That's why she started me with singing. She wanted me to have strong lungs. She normally works in the open air to make bricks and find ore, but this mine put her underground. There isn't enough air flowing through. Then she's been working to clear out the green pool to make it into a bay viewing room."

"How would that work?" Mothy asked, mimicking Wolflock's typical inquisitive chin pinch. "I know how, but for the benefit of my colleague."

Wolflock stared at him with threatening wide eyes, but resumed his dopey, bubbly smile when Girid turned back to him.

"Well, after we clear the pool, ma was going to sell the copper and pay for a wizard and glass maker to put in thick windows so people could see the bay and the mermaids. She wants to turn this mine into a tourist attraction. It's easier than mining and secures her retirement."

"Wouldn't the mine itself secure her retirement? Copper is a highly sought-after metal," Wolflock asked, forgetting his part of the charade.

"Oh... yes... it is..." Girid flushed pink in the light, averting her gaze.

With her eyes off them, Wolflock gestured for Mothy to ask about the lack of a ring on her finger with vigorous hand motions. Mothy frowned, confused.

"Ah... I see. Your hand... It's... It has fingers..." he fumbled.

"Well spotted, my good doctor! It is customary, uh... I mean, do you trade rings when you're engaged to someone in Shiriling?" Wolflock urged.

"Huh? You know about Najord? Are you a friend of his?"

They both shook their heads.

Girid heaved a sigh and let her arms slump. "I suppose everyone is going to find out soon, anyway. Mother broke off our engagement when she found the first copper vein in the mine. For generations, their family has married tradesfolk from town as a sort of 'gift' to the family because it elevates their status. I never cared about that, but after pa passed away, ma was constantly looking for ways to make sure my future was secured and so I wouldn't have to work. We were engaged for just under a year. I guess it was so long because we never really spoke much. Najord is a hard person to like. He loved my singing, but the moment I stopped, he would become cold and rude again. Ma said she'd be my patron, so I didn't have to worry about labouring, and I could sing for my living. I already get a good few deimas from my performances in the local inns, taverns and festivals, but it's my dream to sing a real concert in Mystentine."

Girid's eyes glazed over with the pleasant thought as Wolflock's mind raced.

"Who else has been in the mine since your mother purchased it?" he asked, pinching his chin between his thumb and index finger.

"Huh? Oh, Lord Therym and Najord came down. I put on a performance for them because the acoustics are so enchanting. When ma's health declined, Lord Therym offered to buy the mine from her, but she's very stubborn. She doesn't believe he will extract the copper carefully enough."

"What do you mean?" Mothy asked, mimicking Wolflock's chin pinching.

"Well, ma was trained in the ancient ways of mining. It's a delicate process that removes the ore and replaces it with something of equal worth, density or that which nourishes the ground. It keeps the land stable and restores harmony to the mine."

"Like dressing a wound, but from the land," Mothy hummed thoughtfully.

"Yes! Yes exactly! It's said that ma's lessons came from the Svartálfar themselves."

Mothy and Wolflock both looked at each other when she said the strange word.

"Umm..."

"Oh! Sorry. Svartálfar are an ancient race that live deep underground. Their skin is made from living gems and metals, and they can make metals."

"Don't you mean find metals?" Wolflock asked with a frown, "You can't make metal. That would be like making a pure element."

"I don't know, but that's what they're said to do. They're spoken about only in myths now, but I believe they're real. Part of the reason I sing in the mine is that I hope the Svartálfar will bless the ground and keep it safe, so it doesn't collapse on ma again."

"Again?" Wolflock said sharply.

"She had the Southeast exit collapse on her last week. That's part of the reason she has a cough. Her chest is still bruised, and it hurts to breathe."

"Show me where the collapse happened."

Wolflock dropped his bubbly façade as the three of them headed down the Southeast tunnel towards the bay. Girid took a flaming torch from the auditorium and led the way through the winding, rough-cut stairs. As they came upon the wreckage, Wolflock noticed a breeze was still seeping through the rocks. They were close to the exit. He could even see pin pricks of daylight leaking through.

"Vanmoinen refused to help ma set braces up after... after she got this place. He sold her faulty wood, and it collapsed. She barely escaped with her life." Girid whispered coldly.

Wolflock dusted dirt off the rocks and began shifting them, testing each one to make sure it wasn't holding up another portion of the roof. The same scratch marks from the first entrance were here, as well.

"How does your mother test for what is in the stone?" he asked, finding more white scratches with green centres.

"She uses scrying magic. Why?"

"Someone has been through here that hasn't used scrying magic. They had to carve through it the old-fashioned way." The rocks had the same bubbly texture the geodes had. Mothy helped move the stones aside until they found the planks of wood used to brace the tunnel. He ran his hands over them in the dim torchlight, trying to keep his eyes focused in the darkness so he didn't mistake shadows for clues.

The wood was an exceptional pine. Sturdy, heavy, not a splinter in sight. Yet, the assembly was of the same shoddy quality the first entrance had been. Jaxarna certainly was not a carpenter by any degree. As they dug through, the tunnel held itself together and sunlight washed in. They found the five pieces of wood used to brace the tunnel, and Wolflock laid them out. The nails holding them together were shallow and bent, and the wood had many hammer marks from missing the nail head. His eyes ran over the bracket of the brace. The trapezium shaped piece that held the corner steady had a deep scratch mark over it. As if someone had tried to yank it free, but their implement had slipped. A hooked implement.

Wolflock knelt down, staring at the wooden planks, letting the evidence piece itself together in his mental web. Was it possible that Vanmoinen the carpenter had been down here, and no one had seen? He would know how to pull apart a slipshod brace for sure. But what if it wasn't him? What if it was someone who knew the worth of the green stone a mere inch under the bubbly rock? A noble connoisseur of wealth who may be upset they wouldn't have a mine in their portfolio ever since a certain separation...

"It looks like we need to ask Vanmoinen why his wood wasn't up to scratch," Mothy chuckled at his own joke as he ran his hand along the rough line Wolflock stared at.

"Perhaps... But I think Lord Therym may be able to tell us a bit more right now."

CHAPTER 6

Dirty Dealings

Without another word, Wolflock turned back through the dark caves and followed the path that Dr Qwan and Jaxarna had disappeared into. Girid and Mothy chased behind him, the torchlight dimming as the wind weakened it. They emerged outside on the grassy hill, seeing the doctor and brick maker sitting on a circle of grey stones.

"Are you feeling better?" Mothy asked, walking up to sit beside Dr Qwan.

"Yes. Fine, thanks for asking," the doctor

answered.

Jaxarna laughed through her nose. "I'm fine, lad. Thank you for the concern. Just a coughing fit is all. A bit of fresh air makes it pass easily."

"Would that green water have anything to do with your current condition?" Wolflock queried. It was an odd enough phenomenon that it had to be relevant.

"The magic water? Gods, no. I don't know why it's green, but it's perfectly safe. I've been swimming in it for years. Even drink it when I don't want to come outside while I'm working."

"Mmm... Maybe stop that until we test it, na?" Dr Qwan said with a Xiayahn lilt.

"How about that kit you spoke about in front of the mayor?" Wolflock suggested, irritated that the doctor hadn't already done it. He thought that was why he had been gone for so long.

"Oh yes. Let me get my bits." The doctor started fishing through his pockets until he drew out the vial of powder and a flat box. He opened the small wooden box, and it popped up with six vials, two of which were filled with brown water. "Here." He passed four empty ones to Mothy. "Fetch two vials from the central pool and two from the place where the bay water creeps in."

Mothy dashed away, but Dr Qwan only had the

chance to say, "So... How has that weather been? Surprising, right?" before Mothy had returned.

The doctor set the small vials in the case again and tapped a pinch of the white powder into each of the six bottles and recorked them. Wolflock waited with bated breath for the result.

"Well, that's it for now!" Qwan laughed and snapped the case shut. "I'll let you know the results in a few hours."

"Hours?" Wolflock frowned. "We can't wait that long."

"You're going to have to, Mr Wolflock Felen. Science takes time. This isn't a litmus test. There are no instant results when it comes to these types of things. Not unless you want a false reading. Now, Jaxa, I want you to stay home today. Get more rest. No more work. If I come back and see you working, I will be very upset and have to tell Charma-mama."

"You know, I worry more about upsetting your wife than you. I'll be good and rest today. Besides, I want to see the festival tonight."

"Very good. Charma will be happy."

Redirecting his impatience, Wolflock stood up straight. "Dr Qwan, I've finished my inquiry in the mines thus far. If you're prepared to go, I would like directions to the Lord Therym's house and the Mermaid's Paddle Inn." Wolflock's stern voice surprised Girid so much she fumbled with the torch as she tried to put it into the sconce.

"Certainly, Mr Wolflock Felen. I have pledged my services to you." Dr Qwan bowed deeply, swirling his hands.

Jaxarna and Mothy both snorted.

Wolflock rolled his eyes. If the doctor refused to stop joking around, he would have to do what he did with Mothy. Concede.

"Very good. Let's away, then!"

Mothy bid goodbye to Girid and Jaxarna as Wolflock walked back down the hill. Dr Qwan caught up with them, wrapping his gangly arms around their shoulders. "Mermaid's Paddle, you said? I didn't pick you both for big burly sailors."

"It was recommended by our captain. I believe he had our bags taken there," Mothy grinned.

"Well, if we wanted a lunch, they do the best lobster stew in all of Creast."

"I don't think we'll have time for lunch. I have a suspicion Lord Therym may take up more time than he deserves," Wolflock said darkly.

"If I didn't know any better, I would say you've

taken an instant dislike for the good Lord," Dr Qwan smirked as they made their way through the decorated streets.

"I don't like local nobility having such a powerful voice in the ear of powerful politicians. There's an element of self-serving deception I could never abide by."

"But you are nobility yourself, aren't you?"

Wolflock made a distasteful face. "I suppose. I never enjoyed the unearned privilege, though. Part of the reason they sent me... I mean, part of the reason I left was because of making a few disgruntled local council folk admit their misdealings. My father raised me to know my position was one of power, but that was only to be used to better the community as a whole, not for any nefarious or selfish gains. I may ask for supplies and solitude, but I would assume it is nothing others couldn't also ask for."

Mothy beamed at him as they came up upon a broad inn with a sign that looked like the front of a ship with a mermaid holding an oar.

"Pretty sentiment, Mr Wolflock Felen, but I wonder if you've seen everything about the situation or you're projecting your own ills onto another you see your reflection in?"

"I beg your pardon?"

"Oh, nothing. Just an old Xiayahn proverb. Chosin

is the proprietor of the Mermaid's Paddle. There are five inns in Creast, but this is definitely the sailor's favourite."

Dr Qwan opened the stained-glass doors depicting a squid and crab in battle, and a raucous noise erupted into the street. The three of them squeezed into the tavern part of the inn amongst what looked like a hundred sailors. Mostly without shoes, several were arm wrestling, while others gorged on large portions stacked on their tables. A pair of older ladies raced each other to peel large prawns and a buxom woman stood on a table kicking up a gig as she played a hip drum and sang across the room. The crowd jostled the boys all the way to the bar where an old balding man covered in splotchy spots filled tankards with a bitter smelling liquid.

"Ginger beers is all we has on tap for youngin's like yeh."

"Chosin, my good man! How have you been? How's the tooth?"

Chosin chortled and tucked his bottom lip behind a single canine. "Hard as steel, doc. Hard as steel. How's the missus?

"Hard as steel, barman, hard as steel."

"Who're yeh friends?"

"This is Mothy and Mr-"

"Captain Blutro recommended us come stay here.

From the Silver Ice Hair?" Wolflock cut in, not wanting another formal introduction. "It may be under the name Felen or Enitnelav?"

"Ah, yeah. Yeah, I gots yeh room. Cap'in asked me to make sure the bottle o' ink was all yeh wanted ta pay for it."

"Bottle of ink?"

"Mmm hmm. This 'un." Chosin drew out a delicately curved bottle of onyx ink with a beautiful black label and gold borders. The words "Volfschaf Inte" printed neatly next to an embossed sheep that seemed to be howling at the moon.

"Ah! Yes. Of course. I mean, if that's all you'd like for the rooms, then be my guest."

"Nah, I reckon you're mine. This is fine ink. You've written with it?"

"It's really all we use in Plugh. It's the processed lanolin of the wolf-sheep. Carnivorous sheep. Some people believe they're vampiric sheep, but I just think they were sick of being hunted." Wolflock shrugged as Chosin began writing him a receipt, enamoured by how smoothly it slipped off the quill.

"Nothing like that blubber stuff. And I can write near a whole half page a'fore it runs out. From one dip! From one dip!"

"Just make sure you keep it away from any white linen. It's used to dye fabrics, and it never comes out," Wolflock smiled as Chosin pushed his sleeves further past his elbows before putting his newly treasured ink away.

"So, will you boys be partaking in the festivities this evening?"

"Absolutely," Mothy chimed in, eyeing off the food through the opening to the kitchen. "Tomorrow we're off to Mystentine. We got to join someone in the last carriage."

"Yes. We'll have to be off first thing in the morning, which is why we need to finish looking into the murky bay as soon as possible. May I have our key, Mr Chosin?"

The old barman scratched his chin, leaving a black smudge on it as he looked through the keys on a large ring hanging from his belt.

"There it is. Upstairs, the door on the landing. S'got a shark head mounted above it."

Wolflock led the way to a set of stairs and quickly found their room on the landing between staircases. Seashells and blue glass intricately decorated the pale wood door. The room itself had a small bathroom area with a stone tub and two pristine white beds on either side of a window overlooking the street outside. It relieved him to see their belongings placed at the foot of their beds. Mothy's large rucksack leaned against the white wooden bed frame, and Wolflock's trunk sat neatly and locked at the foot of the other bed. He drew a tiny key from his satchel bag and unlocked the case with a snap. The latches flicked back, and he lifted the hard topped trunk to dig through his neatly stored belongings.

All his clothes lay folded on one side and his wet weather coat divided his toiletries, oils, and balms from them. Amongst the less decorative items were his rosewood handled magnifying glass, a jar of kitchen ash from the Silver Ice Hair, and his leather roll of sketching pencils. But not his journal.

After someone had tried to steal his journal, he made sure he kept it on his person at all times. It was over halfway full of all types of stories and clues he had been collecting. Shoe prints, scratch marks, handprints, key items, and parts of people of interest, like their hands or hair. His notebook also journaled everything he said, saw, or thought. Not knowing who had possibly poisoned the stew on the ship, who saw Parihaan at the bottom of the stairs and said nothing, who tried to stab her with a curvy knife, and who had cut his safety line free during the storm that almost drowned him, made him concerned enough to keep these notes in case something happened, and he needed them.

"Very good. Let's go to Lord Therym's house."

Dr Qwan put down the complimentary soap from the bathroom. "This is good soap. Lavender. You'll smell delightful for the festival."

Mothy smelled the soap and nodded approvingly, but Wolflock rolled his eyes and dragged his friend from the room before something could delay them any further.

"Thanks, Chosin! The room is amazing," Mothy called back as Wolflock hauled him through the sea creature engraved doorway.

"Supper is at sundown!" Chosin called after them, but Wolflock had whipped them both out of the door and around the corner, narrowly dodging two men carrying a large carved archway adorned with shining blue glass shaped like waves.

Dr Qwan caught up to them, placing his hands on both their heads and turning them South. After that point, Wolflock let him lead the way to a building that looked as large as the municipal chambers next to Sheckle's Speckled Shackled Hen. Two great wings of the building extended out to the street, lined with wooden railings carved with images of agricultural life. The ridges of the fish scale tiled roof extended far over the awnings, each one shaped into a different farm animal. The three-storied mansion converged horizontally across and, at its middle peak, had two large white horns curling up to the sky. Wolflock wondered if it represented a bull and if the original family had earned their wealth through farming, as the iconography would suggest. All the decorative wood had large cracks throughout it from ageing in temperatures that varied significantly. Dr Qwan led them up the semicircular stone stairs to the grand doors adorned with images of fruit trees and crops.

"What is this shape? I've always loved this shape," Mothy smiled, admiring the half-leaf shaped frame.

"I believe it's called a half or semi vesica piscis. It's a term referencing the shape created by two perfect circles overlapping. There are several mathematical principles that..." Wolflock stopped when he saw Mothy trying to make the shape by crossing the circles made by his middle fingers and thumbs.

"Ah yes, it is a common part of the symbols applied to many forms of religion and spirituality. Mm... Is very pleasing to the eye and is often calming for children and anxious folk. Good to know these things, though, because circles are hard to navigate." Dr Qwan's face grew into a smirk. "Whenever my wife wants to do anything new with the house, I have to do the math for her, otherwise she throws the whole energy off just to be practical."

Wolflock stopped outside the door, blinking in disbelief at the doctor. "You're a mathematician? You?"

"Why do you look so surprised, Mr Wolflock Felen? Geometry and mathematics are the constants Xiayah is built on. Don't you find equations relaxing? It's like poetry for the logical."

"I mean..." he mumbled as they slipped into the front door, "I find it enjoyable. I just didn't expect you to."

Dr Qwan shrugged and looked around to be greeted. Wolflock could only describe the entrance hall as mighty. An expansive empty floor stretched around them with lit fireplaces on either side. The floor wasn't decorated with images and scenes like outside, but just different types of wood, colouring the intended pathways to staircases on either side of the hall. In front of them stood an archway that could have fitted two more of the grand entrance doors, leading through to a dining hall with two storied glass windows looking out over the bay. On either side of the staircases, Wolflock could see doors leading into different hallways and rooms. To the front left door, he could smell something roasting.

Kitchens, pantry, larder. He thought. Upstairs will

*be the sleeping quarters and private rooms, possibly his
private office too.*

Dr Qwan cupped his hands around his mouth to
shout and announce himself, but Wolflock quickly
clapped his hands around the doctor's.

"I said I wanted to come to the Lord Therym's
house," he whispered pointedly. "I didn't say I wanted to
speak to him." He saw Dr Qwan's eyes lift with a grin and
Wolflock released him. "Where would the master of the
house keep his office?"

"As your guide through Creast, I cannot encourage
any law-breaking activities with a good conscience. What
I can say is that the décor of the bedrooms and sleeping
quarters to the left is the best in all of Shiriling. I've
treated several family members of Lord Therym's there
before."

Wolflock nodded slowly and made his way to the
opposite set of stairs. "Where are all the staff?"

"Oh, I suppose they're helping with the festival.
Lord Therym is quite generous like that. Always lending
his people away from his household. I think it's so his son
doesn't have people waiting on him hand and foot. The
boy would never leave otherwise."

"That's Najord, aye?" Mothy asked as he trailed
up behind them.

"Yeah la," Dr Qwan chuckled, adding a Xiayahn speech note, as they emerged into a wide hallway. One side opened onto a long balcony that overlooked a hibernating courtyard, while the two ends of the hallway led into closed doors. They could hear voices coming from the polished red doors to their left.

Wolflock took a step towards the voices, but Mothy grabbed his shoulders, causing him to lose balance and wobble in place.

"What-?"

"The floors are all board. Walk on the carpet. That way it's less likely to creak."

Mothy walked ahead of him, testing the floorboard as he went, and Wolflock followed behind, holding his breath. His cleverness with sneaking around always impressed Wolflock, and he felt grateful for his friend's practical wit. Without a noise, the boys made it to the far door. Dr Qwan copied them, albeit in a more exaggerated fashion.

Wolflock knelt to peek through the large keyhole in the door while Mothy listened through the crack above him. He had the view of a large desk and Lord Therym sitting behind it on a horned chair covered in cowhide. The nobleman spoke in a low tone to a person sitting in a high-backed chair to the side. He couldn't see more than the stranger's long, thin crossed legs and shiny black shoes marked with street dust. Wolflock held his breath with anticipation as he strained to make out what they were saying.

"...Well, of course I had them sent on earlier. With the cold weather the way it's been, we can't afford to have such delicate materials damaged by being stuck in the snow. No, no, Astraxis. I am sure this was the best course of action. I mean, most of the cargo would have died if they'd been left any sooner. There were barely any goats alive when they arrived here."

"You seem to forget you would be responsible for it either way," came a deep, silky voice, that was barely above a whisper. Something about it triggered his memory, but he couldn't tell what.

"Well, what else can I say? You didn't give me special access to any of the goods."

The other voice stayed silent. Wolflock could feel the tension growing between them as Lord Therym shuffled papers from his desk. He had seen other people do that exact same motion when his father wouldn't let them weasel out of their promises. Seeing Therym squirm brought a grin to his face.

"If you had given me a bit more trust, I'm sure I would have been able to-"

"You had your orders. If I find out, you have been poking around-" Wolflock couldn't place where he knew that voice from. It seemed so familiar. If only they'd speak more clearly.

"I was up at Vanmoinen's, but only this morning. Everything looked fine. Nothing to worry about." He heard Therym swallow. Wolflock could tell he was lying from the nervous tone in his voice..

"We have to stick to the plan. There has been enough deviation. I'm sure anyone else would have been pleased with your thoughtfulness."

"Yes... well... What else was I supposed to do? We couldn't have anything injured." Lord Therym spoke as he moved around his desk. Wolflock twisted his neck to change his viewpoint and saw him stroke the dark leaves of a lush plant on his desk.

The stark contrast of the wooden and tanned room around the bright white and blue pot made it seem very out of place.

"I have half a mind to take that with me. I don't appreciate a plan being manipulated without my approval."

"You can't take her! She's so lovely on my desk. I've worked so hard to sprout those seeds. I even memorised your instructions since I can't read

Shellinden script. As instructed, I was the only one to handle her at all. See? I still have your blue bag ready for the flowers-"

"Purple. The purple bag is for the flowers. The blue bag is for the seeds."

Therym stammered, "Can't you see how she loves it here? If you took her now, the Winter would kill her. Sure you have plenty of others in the cargo moving ahead of you?"

The man named Astraxis stayed silent again, making Lord Therym tidy his desk anxiously again. They could hear by the loud shuffling of the papers. "I'm sure you'll catch up to them if you leave tonight."

After a long pause, the man in the chair whispered, "Trying to get rid of me?"

Wolflock and Mothy made a face at each other, feeling the tension grow.

"No! No, nothing like that. You just seemed urgent is all I was meaning. Just trying to keep a healthy business relationship between friends."

The man in the chair turned the chair to his left and stood up out of view of the keyhole. Wolflock had no other clues to his identity besides his thin legs, voice, and shoes.

"Well, you can do that by showing me the registrar

of what else they've sent through you. I'll need to make sure everything is ready to have the cell activated."

"Of course. It's all a bit vague, though. Boxes with numbers. It's all very mysterious to me. I'm so used to knowing the business about everyone and everything. Perhaps if you tell me more, I'll be able to invest in the right direction?"

The other man chuckled. "The proprietor prefers to have the monopoly on the market until they've seen how things will turn out. Even their most trusted circle can't touch it until it's finalised. Delicate work and all."

"Hversu vonbrigdi," Therym sighed, disappointed. Wolflock didn't understand the words Therym said, but he could tell they were a curse by his tone.

They opened another door and departed through it, leaving Mothy and Wolflock to look between themselves with confused and suspicious glances. Dr Qwan stood back, picking at his nails and pretending to not see their eavesdropping.

"I need to see what is in his office. If he has anything to do with the murk in the bay, it's because of a business interest. I can read between the receipts, so to speak. I'll need a distraction though." Wolflock whispered.

"On it. I'll yell out 'blubber' when you need to get out." Mothy nodded with a wide grin on his face.

"Blubber?"

"It's a funny word I don't s'pose I'll use in many conversations."

"Ah!" Dr Qwan said loudly, making them both jump. "Najord! My fine fellow, how are you on this fine day?"

A boy not much older than Wolflock and Mothy emerged from a door down the hallway and approached them with a bored look as he pocketed a silver pen knife and a leather roll of freshly cut pens. His mousy brown hair pressed in a thin sheet across his forehead under a blue cap rimmed with ginger fox fur. His clothes hung loosely over his thin frame, and he would have looked tidy if he didn't slump like an expended jack-in-the-box.

"Doctor." He gave Qwan a lazy nod, eyeing them all at his father's office door. He didn't speak further, he just gestured to the strangers in his home. He made the motion with his right hand as his left held with a stack of sheet music. Wolflock could see the fine paper, even at a distance, with elegant dark borders soaking through to the underside. .

"Huh? Oh! Who are you two?" Dr Qwan gasped in mock surprise.

Wolflock was about to bite back when Mothy started laughing.

"I'm playing. Fear not my young guest." Dr Qwan smirked at Wolflock before turning to Najord. "These are new guests I'm showing around town. Sir Wothy Urglesprite and his good friend, Doctor Mitzy Blu."

It amazed Wolflock at how stupid, yet confident, the doctor's lie was.

"Doctor?" Najord said sceptically as he eyed Mothy over, but didn't extend his hand in any formality. "Bit young to be a doctor, aren't you?"

"I'm in training," Mothy smiled, running his fingers through his soft blond hair.

"Oh." Najord's bored square face was a similar shape to his father's, but he held none of the charm or confidence of Therym. They stood in an awkward silence for a long moment.

"So... umm... sorry to hear about your engagement," Mothy shrugged.

"Hmm? What?" Najord yawned.

"To Girid?"

The blank look on the nobleman's son's face gave no indication of comprehension.

"The brick maker's daughter?"

"Oh. Yes. That. She'll get along fine, I suppose."

His voice had a slow, drawling quality to it. Najord put his hands in his oversized jacket pockets and stared out of the balcony window.

"Will you watch her sing at the festival?" Dr Qwan shrugged, looking bored as well.

"Of course."

Wolflock frowned. "Why 'of course'? Shouldn't you be upset about her breaking the engagement? Don't boys like you normally feel stung to see their previous beloved thriving? I mean, she's a fabulous vocalist. Wouldn't you be seething that she's the star of the show?"

Najord's brown eyes finally flared up to meet Wolflock's, and his jaw stiffened.

"Hardly. I'm only going to make sure she sings them right. I wrote them. They're my songs. I couldn't care less who sings it, as long as it's done the way I intended. I've written six songs in Shell and four in Corlesian. She isn't a native speaker in anything but bumpkin, and I won't have her butcher my poetry."

"And how does your father feel about all that?" Wolflock probed as he wondered how many languages Najord spoke with that tired drawl.

"Oh, he's never cared about music or art. He's too busy making sure he has everyone wrapped around his pinkie. If there's ten pies, he's got a finger and a knuckle in each of them. No doubt he sent all the staff away to make sure his favourite benefactors would have the best decorations... I still haven't had breakfast."

"Najord? Najord, who are you talking to?"

Lord Therym opened the door to his office, obscuring Wolflock from his view. The old man stepped out into the broad hallway and eyed Mothy to his right.

"Doctor Qwan and his..." Wolflock caught Najord's eye and pressed his finger to his lips. He knew this kind of boy. He hoped that the tense relations with his father would spark that rebellious desire to cause some harmless mischief. Najord stared right at him with no change in expression. "...friend. Dr Mitzy Blu, father. When is breakfast going to be ready?" the young noble whined.

Wolflock's shoulders slumped in relief.

"Doctor who? Oh. You weren't introduced as a doctor before."

"I'm in training," Mothy laughed nervously, scratching his earlobe.

"Oh," Lord Therym's tone dropped. "Not a doctor. Najord, I'm very busy. I need to help Miss Girid's mother get more efficient mining practises in place. She's not well, you see."

"Who?" Najord yawned, stretching up his arms. Wolflock noticed he had a leather vest under his baggy shirt. The young nobleman had been going somewhere in disguise. He couldn't help but smile about having done the same once or twice himself.

Lord Therym's smile faltered. "I thought we would go out for lunch. It's going to be such a great-"

"No. I don't think so," Najord drawled, slumping back so far Wolflock thought he might topple over. "Who's available to make us something?"

"I mean... I can ask one of the-"

"Fine. Come have food. The servants work faster when you're there. Doctors, do you want food too?"

"Absolutely!" Mothy broke into a broad smile and led the way to the stairs.

"Let me just make sure Mr-" Wolflock's gut dropped as Lord Therym turned back into his office, but a loud door slammed, and the old man sighed. "Merry part to you too," he grumbled and followed the others back downstairs, trying to engage his son about how he could speed up mining practises with absolutely no detriment.

Once they were out of sight, Wolflock slipped into the office, looking for the man Lord Therym had been talking to. There was no sign of him. Not a stray hair, nor handprints on the arms of the leather chair. Had he been deliberately careful or just reserved?

The office was decorated much the same as the rest of the house. Taxidermied hunting trophies hung high on the walls, their glass eyes staring nobly forward across the room as if everything that went on in there was beneath them. They looked so old and worn that Wolflock could tell Lord Therym and his son had hunted none of them.

He slid along the wall and tested the door handle on the side of the room he'd seen Therym and his companion leave through. It was locked. He could see the key sitting in the keyhole, blocking his vision. He pressed his ear firmly to the door, but heard no movement. No page turning, no pen scratching. He snatched up a piece of paper from the desk and slid it under the door, then carefully poked a fountain pen through the hole, making the heavy key fall onto the paper. There was just enough of a gap to slide the key back through.

Wolflock's face split into a triumphant grin and he unlocked the door. His proud ingenuity faded away when he suddenly faced a boxy hallway lined from floor to ceiling with ledgers. His eyes slid along the shelves until they took in the door at the other end of the storage hallway. The door at the end of the hallway was ajar. Lord Therym's friend had vanished. He had locked the door between the hallway and the office, but left his escape route open.

Wolflock turned to the shelves to see why the stranger had come into the hallway. What business could they have had here? And why did they lock the door between the offices after Therym went back through. The folders and ledgers lining the walls went back decades and he tapped along them to see if any stood out in the last few years. All were neatly filed away. He could make out the dates they referenced, but as he scanned over them he saw the one for the last year was missing. He ran his long fingers along the spines and took one out, opening it to a random page. Boring business notations. Sales registers. Mining stock. Nothing out of the ordinary.

Wolflock knew the ledger could be in one of two places, being actively written in on the Lord's desk, or taken by Mr Astraxis. No one started doing any tax records until after the Ostara festival because the King would never tax people before Winter or before they planned their year's business. He put the key back into the hallway side of the door and paused. Why had Astraxis locked the door after Therym had returned to see who was outside? Had he wanted to stop Therym from finding him as he took the ledger? Had he wanted to slow down anyone who may see him at the house?

Wolflock scowled. Something much bigger was going on here and he itched to pursue it, but he had to think of Himi. Finding the source of the murk in the bay and how to cure it was more pressing. He had to close the door on the questions regarding Astraxis and Lord Therym's nefarious business dealings for now. Unless it related to helping cleanse the bay, he was just going to have to write down the information for later.

He made his way back into the Lord's office and wondered where he would hide any documents he didn't want people to see. Wolflock analysed the elegant furniture in the office and saw an expensive cordial and nectar cabinet, a few dusty bookcases, and decorative tables with odd items strewn across them. Wolflock made his way over and ran his hands over the trinkets. They must be little tokens and gifts from people, as the style was unlike the rest of the house; stone carved statuettes, decorated wooden beads, shells and geodes, all laid neatly across the decorative side table.

Wolflock opened the drawers in the table and found bags of dried herbs, jars of powders and a bottle of amber alcohol. He picked it up and checked the base, but the maker's seal wasn't the eye with the cross through it like on the bottom of the smuggled alcohol on the Silver Ice Hair. It was a stag, and a forest silhouetted in a circle. The label looked more professional, too. Elegant, trimmed gold paper with the same stag and trees in a circle.

Elderwood Wines & Liquors.

He shook his head. He didn't recognise the manufacturer, but they looked legitimate. Their label held all their credentials, addresses, and all the notes that needed to go onto a liquor bottle. Nothing from the side table pointed to sinister operations. Just exorbitant tastes. He carried on to the desk in the centre of the room. Unlike the rest of the room, this was dishevelled. Papers and notebooks were strewn across the entire desk and hung over the edges. Some were rolled up in the white and blue pot, nurturing a lush, dark leafed plant with large purple flower buds on it.

The writing around the rim of the pot was in the native script of Shellinmerth, the country to the South with the finest Arts and History University in all of Puinteyle. There was an abundance of sun and great rolling green hills through Shellinmerth, as well as the castle the royal imperial family had inhabited for over a thousand years. Wolflock couldn't speak Shellinmerth's language, but he knew how to read it. He expected some fancy poem about growth and bounty, or something similar, around the pot. It surprised him to read instructions instead.

Pinch flowers at base. Do not touch eyes before washing with soap. Dry powder and blow only a palmful. Will be instantaneous.

What would be instantaneous? And why would instructions about a flower be around a pot in a language no one in this country would typically be able to read? His web of clues stretched as far as it could, but he couldn't find the connections. There had to be something though. His gut churned in frustration. Therym had stroked the plant and spoken about it. The mysterious Astraxis had given it to him. Given instructions about it to him. Therym didn't strike Wolflock as the leisurely gardening type, so what was so special about this plant and the instructions wrapped around it?

He pinched the bridge of his nose and strained to think about it. After a few minutes he huffed and looked away. Perhaps looking for other clues would help refresh his perspective. He turned his attention to the papers on the desk. Wolflock recognised the many letters of business and trade, but the one in the middle of his workspace seemed out of place. Wolflock expected a fresh note, an unfinished letter, or something dated closer to the current date. Not an invitation to last Mabon's feast. Wolflock lifted the invitation and smirked. Underneath sat a response Lord Therym had been penning before he'd been interrupted by Astraxis. The ink was completely dry, so he hadn't been writing it while he was talking to his visitor, but he had covered it quickly to hide it. The invitation he'd placed over it had smudges and inky imprints on the back. Wolflock read over it to see why Therym tried to hide it from his visitor.

My dear Borso,

I am terribly concerned with the collapse, and I will send funds to help aid the doctors so the miners can be ready to work as soon as they are mended. Please don't leave. I will organise everything to address your worries as soon as I am able. As for your concerns about the new mapping, I assure you that a grid-like structure is still the most efficient method of mining, and we are more likely to find every bit of ore. If we're lucky, we won't miss the gemstones like we did...

It cut off without saying where he had missed

gemstones. Who was Borso? Was he the manager for one of Therym's mines? Perhaps a foreman or a lead builder for his extraction projects? Wolflock dug through the dishevelled papers for more information on the man and quickly spied three grubby notes from the man in question, all complaining about collapses because of the unnatural mining methods Lord Therym was insisting on utilising. Others mentioned the cheaper woods breaking under the strain they were holding up, causing cave-ins. One letter complained of several miners being injured from a poisonous gas that would have been discovered if Therym had sent through the necessary chemistry sets or even a small bird.

Wolflock's mouth twisted in distaste. Why were they mining so deeply the air wasn't fresh? Normal mines throughout Puinteyle were mostly open unless they originated in a cave structure. Was Therym cutting corners and digging too greedily? No wonder Jaxarna didn't want to sell her mine to him. She had followed the natural flow of the caves. Yes, it may lead to less yield, but it wouldn't cost lives or habitat destruction.

He opened the draw and found hundreds of scattered red tickets, all with the same logo. Two pine trees and an axe, all with two hole punches. One hole punch must have been for when the cargo was stored, and a second for when it was removed as a way to prove purchase. The scattered tickets dated back for years as far as Wolflock could see, progressively increasing in frequency until they became every few days. He couldn't find anything within the last two weeks, though. Lord Therym had been moving many wares, but what? If the mining shipments were sent here first and then moved on, that would make sense. As he became more successful, that would have explained the increase in frequency. Then nothing.

The sudden stop left Wolflock feeling suspicious. If he'd seen that Therym had moved all his business elsewhere, there would still be a paper trail for that. But to just completely cease all business, told Wolflock something dramatic had forced Therym to cease his operations. He could feel it in his gut. He was close to the answers. Wolflock's heart beat in his throat. He didn't know how much time he had left to search.

In the draw filled with tickets, Wolflock also found a few pieces of crumpled paper. One was a letter in a furious scrawl that read:

To Therym   Culimpus 26th of Eolas Revari
Year 8th King Rayin,
We are leaving. I don't even want to write your name, it disgusts me so. You've ignored all our wishes

and the mines are no longer safe. We won't work under such conditions. There is always other work to be had. I expect you to send the miner's final pay by next week with damages, or I will take this to the ombudsman.

Borso

The letter's date came from three weeks ago. That explained the drop in needing storage. If the miners weren't working, the ores and gemstones weren't coming in. He then saw one letter from Jaxarna, one from Vanmoinen, and what looked like a reply to Vanmoinen that was cut off.

*Dear Therym,   Lucimpus 1st of Nibit'ling Ickst
                    Year 8th King Rayin,*

We have been friends for many years, and you have helped me thrive, so I don't ask this lightly. Please remove what your friend is storing in my shed. I know I said I'd house it for two months, but I can't. There is a terrible stench coming from it that is attracting predators and scavengers. My boy nearly got mauled by a hungry lion skulking about. If it's poorly stored goat meat, that's bad enough, but I think I heard movement. Whoever you're dealing with isn't telling you the full story, my friend. We didn't agree to house animals, especially ones that weren't being looked after. I know they've paid a lot, but, in good conscience, I can't proceed. I can't condone cruelty. They can have the money back if they need it.

Vanmoinen

The letter was sealed with the two pines and axe symbol and dated for two weeks ago. Wolflock's piercing blue eyes scanned Lord Therym's response.

My good friend Van,
        Lucimpus 2nd of Nibit'ling Ickst
        Year 8th King Rayin,

I can assure you I have seen the cargo and there are no animals there. They have some odd plants that may give off the unpleasant smell, and perhaps they didn't salt the goat meat correctly. They're not from around here, you know? I'll check in with them and see if I can get them cleaned up and moved today. Don't you fret about the money. These people are very wealthy, and I'll let them know their plans have changed...

Caught in the excitement of finding such obvious pieces to the puzzle, Wolflock read the note from Jaxarna, dated just last week.

Therym,

Quintampus 10th Nibit'ling Ickst, 15, Rayin

You must do something. I know Herfed won't help. He wouldn't put his neck out for me after I had a go at him for letting the inns get overbooked last Yule. Vanmoinen's boy has been spying on my mine for his father! I just know he's up to no good. Girid is scared. Make sure he stops coming around. I put the fear of a beating into him, but he keeps coming back. I wouldn't have thought about it at all until Vanmoinen sold me rotten wood. That's what caused the cave in, not poor mining practises. Herfed checked it out and just told me to build better braces. You remember all those rocks falling on my chest? It's still hard to breathe now. It only happened after Vanmoinen started getting jealous of the mine. I know he hates my success, but what am I to do? You have to help me. I know Girid and Najord didn't work out, but we have been friends much longer than that. Please tell me what can be done.

Jax.

So, Jaxarna thinks Vanmoinen was sabotaging her mine and sending his son to spy on her operation. Would he have gone so far as to leech a poison into the bay in order to frame her? Wolflock pocketed the letters. The bay was first infected when the river stopped running two weeks ago. There had been no signs of chemicals or disease leaching into the bay from the mine.

He also couldn't find any evidence that the nobleman Therym had had any direct hand in the diseased bay. He had shady dealings, mysterious meetings and was everyone's 'good friend', but there was nothing concrete. Which meant that Wolflock had to check the lumber mill.

"You can't tell me that wasn't lamb blubber!" Mothy gasped from down the hallway.

Wolflock's eyes shot up to the door. He was out of time.

"No, Mr... uh... Blu," Lord Therym replied, clearly exasperated. "Lambs do not have blubber."

"I mean technically blubber is just better-quality fat. Kind of. My wife would hate to hear me call blubber fat. I believe what my associate is trying to say is that the lamb was so delicious that it could have been mistaken for blubber. Translation error, I'm sure." Dr Qwan prattled with a deliberate volume that Wolflock understood as a warning.

"I thought it was dry and wiry," Najord droned.

"Well, I must get back to work. Merry part, gentleman. Najord, see them out, please." sighed Therym.

"Merry part," Najord answered. Wolflock could visualise him lazily turning to their guests and flicking his hand in farewell to them.

He had no time to think too long about it, though. Mothy had said the code word. He closed the draw and took three long strides to the side door, yanking it open and whipping into the hallway. He heard the main door of the office open just as he closed the hallway door.

He didn't exhale until he was out of the hallway and back into the familiar entrance hall. Mothy and Dr Qwan waved to him as he ran down to them, and they set off at a light jog to get out of Lord Therym's house.

"Any luck?"

Wolflock smirked, pulling out the letters. "Everything points to the lumber mill, no matter how much people want us looking at the mine."

CHAPTER 7

Slimy Source

I see you're not artistically inclined?" Mothy snorted, rolling the corner.

"You've seen my shoe sketches. You know I can draw."

The midday sun dripped through the clouds in a pale shower as Dr Qwan led them through the streets along the Southern most road heading West. Creast's street activity thinned as they reached the edge of the shell-shaped town. The second and third stories of the wooden buildings overhung the road, laced with fluttering streamers tied under their scale awnings.

The three of them passed through the South-West gate out of town and tramped up a road with deep gutters from the weight of the carriages and cargo usually carried along it. The empty river wound between this road and the Northwest one as if it looked for an escape to the sides, before disappearing under the great wooden wall surrounding Creast. As they reached the top of the hill, they took in a thick pine wood forest as far as the eye could see. Nestled a few rows of trees in, was a tall lumber mill with a stationary water wheel.

As they passed through the wide wooden archway, Wolflock noticed the lumber mill was a vast operation. From the hill, he could see groves of trees at different ages clustered together. New saplings pin-cushioned the land to the far South, and, directly West, were much older, established pines.

A breeze caught a torn poster by the entranceway, and Wolflock put his hand on it to see what it said. It revealed a map of the lumbermill with its major landmarks scratched onto it in charcoal. The buildings he saw before him were at the far right of the map and, scattered through little tree patterns drawn on the paper, were the boxes and squares meant to represent the lumber mill. In the distance, beyond the lumber mill and toward the back end of the map, were the large storage sheds. Distinct swirling marks outlined the rivers running through the property.

As he ran his hand over it, he could feel similar patterns in the wood underneath it. He pulled the large map to the side and saw a far more elegantly carved map in the wood beneath. Outlined with native Shiriling cords and interwoven patterns, the symbols of the buildings and houses were far more intricate. Wolflock made a quick sketch of both maps. Mothy came over without a word and held back the first map after seeing his friend struggle to draw in his journal, with his leg propped up as a table.

The tallest building stretched across the banks of the river and it seemed to be where the logs floated down to and were processed into planks or blocks. Except it was dry.

No, Wolflock thought as he looked at the river that was meant to be running a few yards away from where they stood at the map. It's slimy. And it reeks of yeast.

A homestead, with high sloped scale shingled roofs, leaned forward to greet them, happily puffing plumes of smoke from the grey stone chimney. Either the carpenter or his son were in the building, he determined.

Dr Qwan put his hand to his mouth to call out, but Wolflock clamped his hand firmly over the doctor's hand.

"Let's go and have a nose around first, shall we?"

The doctor raised a black eyebrow, shrugged, and gestured for Wolflock to lead the way.

Without a word, they followed the road along the riverbed.

"You can both smell that, yes?" Wolflock asked as the yeasty stench grew.

"The aroma of rotten bread?" Mothy snorted.

"What is that?"

"Well, if I were to hazard a guess," Dr Qwan took a long inhale over the river, "I'd say someone was trying to brew potions of the alcoholic sort. And not for medical purposes either."

"Drinking alcohol?" Wolflock asked.

"Indeed, Mr Wolflock Felen. Beer, to be more precise. Hot beer is a favourite in these areas, as well as mead. But there are strict regulations on the selling and crafting of such things. Too easy to turn into a poison for the body and mind."

"Where are the storage sheds the lumberjack rents out?"

Dr Qwan shrugged. "I rarely use his storage facilities. I get everything sent to my office and home so my wife can check the quality upon arrival."

"So you don't know where it is?"

"Somewhere on the property?"

Wolflock rolled his eyes, but, when he caught Mothy's face, he stopped. His best friend's features hardened.

"Mothy? What are you thinking? Where would you hide an illegal alcohol operation?"

Mothy's hazel eyes scanned across the ground, the trees, the equipment left along the river as they walked on. Wolflock could see that they were in a semi-remote mill with plenty of places to hide nefarious business.

"We're after a medium-sized shed. Nothing too big because that would draw attention. It will be the most average looking place the furthest away it can be. That's where people are less likely to look and disturb things." Wolflock instructed Mothy and Dr Qwan.

After close to half an hour of walking along the hillside, they came across several sheds. The details they passed were repetitive. The regrowing of the trees to provide constant renewable lumber left them all looking the same. By the end of their walk Wolflock felt frustrated that it took so long to get to where they needed to go. Two stories high and large enough to store a year's worth of building materials and lumber in each. Wolflock counted seven sheds in total. He peeked into the doors of the first few to see crates, barrels, and sacks stacked throughout them. Nothing smelled off besides the yeasty smell coming from the river.

Just storage... And none like what Mothy expected to find...

Wolflock continued pacing along the riverbed, pinching his chin between his index finger and thumb, seeing the brown slimy webbing keeping moisture held along the edges of the river. Wolflock looked back at the maps he'd drawn in his journal, following the river with his finger.

"Mothy! Mothy, come look," he shouted. Both the doctor and Mothy jogged over, peering over his shoulder. "There's another building away from these. Quickly!"

He set off at a run, excited to find the mysterious shed. He expected that all the evidence they needed for why and how the bay had been infected would be in there. Even if it was empty, he could find the traces of the clues he needed. He was sure of it.

He rounded the corner and choked.

The last shed laid in a collapsed heap in the middle of the riverbed, damming it up.

Splintered planks and twisted brackets burrowed into the mud, letting no more than a trickle of water through the landslide debris. Mothy and Dr Qwan caught up, only to stop, speechless, at the catastrophic blockage.

Wolflock flung out his arms and stopped them both from taking another step.

"Let me see your shoes."

He committed the prints of their shoes to memory, even though he knew Mothy's shoes would smudge with every step. The value of knowing who had trod where meant that by process of elimination, he'd always have the data he needed to know where people had been and in what order. Mothy's unique way of walking in order to smudge his footprints left just as a unique impression as if he'd had personally designed shoes. They followed him around as he bent over, magnifying glass to the ground, hunting for clues. Shoe prints, hand prints, jewellery or trinkets, anything to identify the people who had been here and more about what they had been doing.

He identified two similar sets of shoes in the clay-like mud. Sturdy work boots with a deep tread. Likely to be lumberjack boots.

Vanmoinen and his son knew about this. They had been here. The boots went right up to the edge of the debris.

Some planks had similar boot prints as well as little smears of blood on them. *They thought they could clear it, but the wood splintered, and they left it. But why?*

Deep tracks carved from where the door had been

led back down the road. Judging by the layers in which the drag marks to and from the wagon appeared, Wolflock could tell several details. Very heavy crates had been dragged in, but they had dragged out sacks. No... not sacks... the distinct parallel lines of heels. He held his breath as his blood ran cold. They had dragged bodies from here. Dead or alive was the question.

This was huge.

This was the reason the carpenter and Therym had been lying. Therym knew something was wrong. Vanmoinen had asked for things to be moved out of a warehouse and Wolflock would have bet his favourite shoes it had been this one.

He could see that they had left in a hurry. Maybe they hadn't been able to secure the same wagon that brought them here? He could tell because the drag marks overlapped the first wagon, but not the second one's tracks. The marks of the second wagon leading away through the mud came from a strange beast with pointed hooves. Wolflock wondered for a moment what kind of Shiriling beast could make tracks like that and he felt a chill from how deep they cut into the ground. They nearly looked horse-like, but the jagged point looked like a strange claw. His attention returned to the rubble as the tracks lead back to the entrance of the lumber mill.

He walked around the perimeter of the wreckage, finding scraps of light debris blown by the breeze. Strands of hair, dust, leaves, and paper caught on damp grass around the shattered wood. He found one of the biggest intact pieces of paper, but it identified no one and just spoke of not releasing anymore of something to someone until they paid double because of their attitude.

The only other interesting piece of paper was the corner of a burnt sheet that had a beautifully designed border that soaked through to the underside. The elegant flourishes looked like the designs he had seen on sheet music.

Eventually he climbed carefully onto the destroyed shack, getting what felt like a solid footing and started pulling back sheets of roofing. The doctor and Mothy helped him shift shattered beams, and then a new stench hit them.

They lifted a large piece of roofing off to find a crushed, blackened metal tub and thick bent metal poles welded into what looked like a bent and twisted cage. Along with the fermenting beer stinging their nostrils, the ammonia from human waste assaulted them. Mothy and Wolflock gagged, and Dr Qwan let out a noise of disgust.

Unable to take it, Wolflock stepped back, but the unstable wood slid, and he toppled backwards, landing hard on his side, and rolling into the slimy riverbed. The smell stung his eyes, and he felt the slimy webbing prickle his skin. His eyes watered as he tried to hold his breath and scrambled out of the slippery riverbed.

He reached the top, wiping mud from his face, only to face a smiling Dr Qwan.

"Well, that just won't do, Mr Wolflock Felen. Clean up now."

"Huh?"

Wolflock saw the doctor raise his foot and before he knew it, he was soaring backwards. He landed, with a splash, in the river, floundering for a second before he scowled up at the doctor, then wished he hadn't as clean water rushed into his mouth and nostrils. The fresh pine oils felt refreshing, even through the indignity of being kicked into the river. He swam back through the chilling water to the edge, glaring up at the doctor as he grabbed tufts of grass to pull himself back onto the bank.

"Did you see that, doctor?" Mothy ran forward to pull Wolflock out of the water.

"I most certainly did. How interesting... Let me get some samples!"

Wolflock looked daggers at the doctor, kneeling down to collect the overflowing water from the river. The rich green grass contrasted with the doctor's white coat and the lock of golden hair the doctor was standing on.

Feeling vindictive, the young man had no qualms pushing the doctor over into the river in order to retrieve the hair before he accidentally damaged it. Dr Qwan didn't become submerged in the water, but rather just fell in the shallows, keeping everything but his behind and left arm dry.

"I will pretend that was to get a more thorough sample of the water," he said warningly as Mothy helped him up, watching Wolflock with a nervous smile.

"You were standing on this." He held up the strands of hair with smug satisfaction.

Dr Qwan leaned down and sniffed at them. "Ah yes. Hair. Of the human variety, I suppose."

"Except look closer."

Dark purple flecks dusted the golden hairs.

"What on Pelaia..." the doctor snatched the hairs up and pulled them taunt before his eyes.

Wolflock had already set about again with his magnifying glass to the ground, following a trail of purple dust on the grass and wood scraps. Some clumps had dried after the water coagulated them, but he found the largest amount of it right at the back of the shed, where the wood looked chipped and worn, rather than the freshly splintered pieces that lay shattered in the shed wreckage. The purple dust coated the wood like fine paint. It also covered a roughly made metal file, scratched from being used and thrown aside just outside of the shed.

Someone had been in that cage, he thought as a chill gripped his throat. They had planned an escape, only to come into contact with this purple dust. They had gotten to the river. Had they made it any further? Not everyone had escaped, if anyone had. The drag marks at the entrance of the shed prove that.

His eyes moved along the back of the shed to the riverbed. The thin streams of human filth had seeped into the river, as well as the waste from the beer. They were dried and he guessed that they came from two weeks ago when the shed had been destroyed. Had the captive people been ill? Was that the sickness that was now in the bay? Was Vanmoinen aware of this? Had he been complicit in these evil dealings? Was he trying to shift suspicion back onto Jaxarna to protect himself?

Wolflock heaved up the broken wood, discerning the different types from the building and the cargo within. Broken barrels still maintained a bowed shape, even though they were shattered free of their rings. Crates clung to their nailed edges and had broad thin pieces that acted as walls.

Wolflock dug through the wreckage, looking for makers' seals, trying to find out the identity of the agents who treated people like cargo. Most of the crates, boxes and barrels were unmarked, making them suspicious enough, but, eventually, he came upon a small box of broken bottles. He picked up a large shard and sniffed it. The familiar sting of alcohol attacked his nostrils, and he carefully sifted through the broken glass and crate fragments for the bottom of a bottle. It only took him a moment to find one and underneath was the familiar eye shape with the X through it.

Without hesitation, he looked up to find Mothy. His gut twisted. How would his friend react? Would it make him more determined to help solve the case? Would it terrify him and cause him to shut up like a clam? He didn't know.

He threw the glass aside, knocking it against what looked like an upturned crate. He hadn't looked underneath the containers, but seeing the base of this one made him realise he had to get Mothy away from the shed. Underneath the broken crate was a huge burnt eye and X smeared with the same purple dust.

Mothy looked up at him and waved. "Lockie! You need to see this."

Happy for the excuse to move away from the

chilling scene, Wolflock carefully manoeuvered over the debris, back to his friend and the doctor. Before he finished his expedition, he heard the sound of many feet galloping on dirt.

"Ay! What are you doing? Get off that! Get out of here!"

Vanmoinen rode down the lane on a huge black headed elk, bearing towards them with gigantic branching antlers. A second man rode behind him on a similar gigantic beast.

"Ah! Mr Carpenter," Dr Qwan addressed the red-faced Vanmoinen incorrectly. "I was just showing my associates what used to be a beautiful river, and we had to know why the frost had taken it so early this season."

Vanmoinen and the other man got down from their elks and stormed towards the three.

"I was just commenting on how strange it is that ice should be wood this year. And I could have sworn you used to have a shed here, did you not? I hope the new wood ice didn't claim it as well."

Wolflock and Mothy both snorted at the doctor's nonchalant remarks.

"Wood ice!?" Vanmoinen roared, glancing around for a reason to be righteously mad at them and not just afraid they'd discovered his secret. "You've destroyed my shed! You've ruined it and blocked the river!"

"Is that what you're going for now?" Wolflock scoffed. "After you told everyone the river froze over because the gods were displeased at Jaxarna's mine?"

"I-I-I only said that because I didn't know you had destroyed my shed!" he stammered.

"Two weeks before we arrived here?"

"You could have conspired with the doctor here for weeks before any of this!"

"To what end?" Wolflock waved his hand at the mess before them.

"How am I to know the workings of such vagrants!?"

"Well, we've done you a service, my wood-working friend." Dr Qwan drew a tiny device that looked like a telescope pointing down to a glass panel he had placed the hair on with the purple powder.

Everyone stared at the doctor as he twisted the knobs on his device, pressing his eye to the telescope part. Wolflock's eyes brightened with intrigue as he watched the doctor.

"W-what do you mean?" Vanmoinen's voice shook like a leaf as he and the man Wolflock supposed was his son drew nearer, their anger dissipating as their curiosity grew.

"May I?" Wolflock held out his hand, into which the doctor passed the contraption.

"As you'll see there, that is the pollen and powder of the plant found only in the hot, wet regions of the continent, Dominia Mendis Impertio, commonly known as Lady Mind Master. Also known as Gnome Hats. Also known as Death Bells. Also known as-"

"We get it. What am I seeing? Is that the hair?" Wolflock waved at the chattering doctor to make his point as he stared at the jagged edged translucent blonde hair covered in large purple and green fluff balls.

"That indeed, Mr Wolflock Felen, is a hair. But, more importantly, that plant found on the hair is commonly used as an anaesthetic for eye surgery. It numbs pain, but also blinds patients for approximately three days. It's lethal in doses slightly larger than those of the analgesic quality, and also has been known to induce memory loss and make patients highly susceptible to suggestions."

"But we found that everywhere here?" Mothy frowned, taking a step away from the shed.

"That's right, Dr Mothy."

Wolflock could have looked through the inverted telescope for hours, but he heard the silence after Dr

Qwan finished speaking and knew he had to give his own explanation.

"So, if we destroyed your shed two weeks ago, Dr Qwan would only have done it so you weren't under the power of people trading in mind controlling drugs, illegal alcohol, and slaves. All of which we have found evidence for here today. Of course, if you'd like to dispute that as well, I have the tickets you signed for these people to have storage in this shed right here." He drew the ticket nubs he'd found in Therym's draw.

Vanmoinen's skin lost all colour.

"Father?" His son placed a shovel-like hand on the older man's shoulder. "What are they talking about? I thought this shed was empty. You told me Girid was lying."

The carpenter choked, looking back and forth between their faces. For a moment, Wolflock thought he may run. Then he fell to his knees, gripping short, dark hair as his face twisted in anguish.

"I didn't know... I didn't think I needed to know. I came down to make sure they didn't set it on fire or anything, and I could only smell something terrible. Thought since it was out of the way, it wasn't an issue, but the smell got worse. I asked Therym to tell them to leave. They left in a big hurry and, when I came down to clean up and see what was making the smell, I found this."

He sobbed as he motioned to the shed and river.

"Why didn't you tell the mayor? Why didn't you tell anyone?" Wolflock frowned.

"I couldn't... I couldn't risk the mill's reputation like that. If the people knew I caused all the sickness in town, I'd be forced to leave forever. My son would be disgraced. I didn't want to sell my land, but now it might be the only alternative. I don't want to wash the disease into town and risk hurting anyone else, but I can't do my work if the mill isn't running on the water."

"I'll keep working on this," Dr Qwan placed a drop of the vials pertaining to the infected bay water on the glass of his inverted telescope, "and we'll see if we can find a way to cure the disease. Then we'll open up the river when we know it's safe, aye?"

Vanmoinen stood up, wiping fine wood shavings from his arms, as he nodded doubtfully.

"We will have to tell the mayor, though. I think it's only right. Jaxarna hasn't caused the sickness and her name must be cleared, even if we're not ready to restore the river yet," Mothy interjected as Wolflock and the doctor pondered the information they had collected.

"Very well. If we can keep this quiet, I will be forever in your debt. Oh," Vanmoinen added as they began walking back down the road to the mill, "don't touch the brown slime, otherwise you'll feel horrible in just a few minutes."

Wolflock was too deep in thought to pay much heed to his warning. He had no intention of falling into the riverbed again. They made it back to the lumber mill entrance when he realised Mothy had been staring at him with wide blue eyes the entire way.

"What?"

"You're not sick, are you? Queasy? Chilly? Aches and pains? Let me see your tongue?" Mothy tried to open Wolflock's lips to see inside his mouth, but he smacked his hands away, affronted.

"Stop. No. I'm fine. Why? Huh... I see... Curious..." he mumbled to himself. "I'm not sick. Yet I was covered in the stuff. Maybe it's only infectious if you ingest it."

"Nope," Dr Qwan made them both start as he talked into his scope. "Even being near it makes some people ill. I think you're not ill because we washed it off you right away. Mothy and I both saw it. All covered in brown slime, then, like magic, nothing. Clean as a whistle."

"Whistles aren't clean. They're filled with saliva." Wolflock rolled his eyes as they made it back into Creast and headed towards the municipal building.

"Mmm... You say that, but the sound is clean."

"If it washed off me, then why not just open the river and let it wash it all off?"

Mothy continued to stare between the two of them as they spoke.

"We don't know how it will react when the freshwater and saltwater mix. It may create the perfect environment for it to grow beyond the bay, and that would mean the entire sea is in trouble. Let me finish a few more tests and then we'll see if it's ok."

Wolflock chewed his cheek. He knew the doctor was right, but he couldn't help worrying that, if they took too long, Himi and her family, or, at least, her kind, would be in danger of becoming ill, too. Without more data, he couldn't act. The risk was too great.

They made their way to the council building to find men and women rushing about, their arms stacked with papers, all wearing the same side buttoned, high-necked coat. The building itself was just as grandiose as Lord Therym's house, with images of battles, monsters, fishing, mermaids, and forests carved into every inch of the walls, columns, and floors. It was a collage of history, interspersed with cabinets and portraits. A stern woman sat behind the main counter, her blonde hair braided tightly around her head and her sharp face pointing people in the direction they needed to go.

Various staff ran up to her, spilling a breathless question onto her desk, and she responded with only six or less words, sending them running off again. The cool, calm efficiency impressed Wolflock.

"We need to speak with Mayor Merlai as a matter of great urgency," he said as he rested an arm on her desk, hoping to get through by being different to everyone else racing around.

Her dark eyes narrowed as she looked down at him.

"Appointment?"

"No. He won't want one for this."

"Blackmail?" she squawked, a bit too pointedly for Wolflock's liking.

"N-no! Nothing like that. It's about the infection in the bay."

"He's not here." She slammed a stamp down on a document handed to her by a squat little man, who raced away before the ink had time to dry.

"Where is he then?"

She handed three folders to another man who ran up, so bulky his muscles threatened to tear his jacket arms. "He had business at the bay. He has no appointments for today. You are welcome to wait and catch him between appointments if he comes back for the day."

"Oh! Silly me," Dr Qwan chuckled, pulling out three brown paper bags of herbs and shaking them. "I was meant to drop this off for him. He needed a refill. Do you mind if we just pop through and save you the flight, Alkonost?"

The receptionist chuckled like she had a mouth full of rocks. "Fine. Be quick. And take nothing."

"Of course, of course," Dr Qwan answered as he drew Wolflock and Mothy away.

Wolflock tore his arm free and ran back to the desk. "What would you have said if I said it was blackmail?" He had to know.

Alkonost smiled widely, making her face more bird-like. "We have procedures for that." She blinked and Wolflock could have sworn her eyes changed to a fiery yellow, but they returned to their dark intelligent focus a moment later. An unsettling curiosity crept up inside him. He wanted to follow it and ask more questions, but thought better of it.

With a nod, he caught up with the others in the mayor's office. Considering the grandeur of the rest of the building, the mayor's office was quite humble. Fairly plain, with simple walls and portraits of previous leaders circling the room, he had only a few personal effects on his desk, such as a lady's locket open with a child and the mayor's cameo, and a little box of perfumes. Wolflock noticed that the perfume box had one missing, and the others were mostly empty. The only other notable thing about the room was the seven hooks with seven different coats hanging from them.

"Does the mayor wear a different coat on different days of the quarter moon?" Wolflock asked, looking over the coats and checking their pockets. All were empty and clean except for the second.

"Oh yes," Dr Qwan smirked. "It's how he remembers what day it is and what meetings he needs to attend."

"Fool... Oh? Mothy, look at this." He beckoned his friend over and showed him the folds of the collar on the second coat.

"Purple powder. But how?"

"Is this his Lucimpus or Sidumpus day coat?"

"The first day of the week is Relimpus, so that must be today's coat. Lucimpus. I thought you would know that Mr clever Wolflock Felen." Dr Qwan walked closer to examine the purple powder alongside them.

"Some people don't treat the weekends as the start

of the week."

"Oh, our Mr Mayor doesn't have days off."

"Was he wearing this coat at all today?" Wolflock asked, finding the purple powder only across the front of the collar and shoulders.

"No. The festival has thrown out his schedule. He normally comes in and puts on his coat, collects his meeting notes and heads out, but I didn't see him with it on at Sheckle's, so he hadn't been in. I'm sure Alkonost could confirm. Why do you ask?"

"Because the last time he would have worn his coat is on the last Lucimpus when he had a meeting with Lord Therym in his office. The same place where we saw the purple plant."

Dr Qwan scratched his thin black beard and moved to the desk in thought. "That sounds right, but you didn't see any purple powder in the room, did you?"

"No. It was spotless."

"Well, then... Ah! What's this?" Dr Qwan saw the open case of perfumes with one missing. "Ah. I knew he was out. The mayor hasn't been taking his medication."

"If he's out, how do you know he hasn't been taking it?" Wolflock asked as he saw a geode on the desk with a strange green slice through it.

"Because this anti-nausea medication makes you

drowsy if you take too much. Our dear mayor hasn't been a sleepy fellow lately. Oh, no. He's been collecting nausea medication for someone else. Someone much larger than him if he's already through it. Much larger indeed."

"I don't know about the person he's getting medication for or why, but I have an idea of where he's gone." Wolflock held up the geode, green streak out.

"Jaxarna's mine?" Mothy frowned, confused. "But why?"

"Let's go and find out."

The early afternoon sun finally made its way through the clouds as they jogged to the mine again. Tourists filled the streets and the tired locals looked relieved to have some business to distract themselves, but comments about the murkiness of the bay weakened their resolve. The decorations that were draped over the steep roofs rustled in the breeze, and any mermaid decorations were painted with bright watercolours to make them stand out.

They ducked between the maintenance folk, who were putting more oil into the street lanterns hanging from half arched, carved wooden poles. The three of them made their way through the beautiful coastal town to the grassy knoll leading to the mine. Dr Qwan continued to look through his scope at the different samples of water, strapping his device to his chest, as he walked behind them.

It wasn't long before they reached the mine and listened. Jaxarna and Girid had gone home for the day, as was clear by the extinguished torches, so any noise they heard had to be Mayor Merlai.

Wolflock took out Dr Qwan's lighter and led the way into the cavern. They came to the main auditorium and stopped, listening again. At first, they heard nothing, but, after a few moments, they heard someone groaning from the tunnel leading down to the bay.

Wolflock motioned for them to be silent as they began their descent into the tunnel. It wound around itself like a spiral ramp and the air grew dense with moisture. In the dim white light of the flame, Wolflock held his breath, trying not to make a sound. The groaning turned into worrisome moans, and he could hear shoes stamping back and forth across hard stone and soft sand or silt. A thick, fishy stench mixed with the air. Seaweed, salt, and something else created a wall a less curious being would refuse to pass.

The white light cut along the edge of their tunnel as it flared out into a cavern, being lapped by the rocking waves of the bay. Wolflock lifted the lighter higher, seeing plates and bowls strewn all over the rocky ground. Each were filled with all manner of rotting food and drink, adding to the stench engulfing them. Wolflock pinched his nose and covered his mouth with his right hand as he stepped into the cave.

A shaking lump about the size of Mayor Merlai rocked back and forth before a large stone slab next to an oil lantern. Atop the stone lay a deathly still merman, with an enormous belly distended beyond Wolflock's height, yet his tail and arms emaciated. The normally blubbery merfolk looked as if he'd been starved for weeks.

The shaking lump in front of him let out a low sob that droned on until Wolflock moved to step forward, kicking a shard of loose rock.

"Who's there?" the mayor barked. He snatched up his lantern and flung his other arm out.

Wolflock and the others stayed silent, as the ginger bearded man looked quite deranged. His hair clung to his damp brow and his blue eyes bulged with anxiety.

"Who's there I say!" he roared again, this time brandishing a knife. He waved his arm, slashing right near Wolflock's chest.

Rhiannon D. Elton

CHAPTER 8

The Mayor & the Mermaid

Come out where I can see you-ack!"

The mayor buckled forward, clutching his chest as he fell into a violent coughing fit. Wolflock glimpsed the 'knife' and started laughing. He relit the match and stepped forward past the mayor to begin looking over the merman.

"Get-ack-away from him," Mayor Merlai wheezed.

"He's no danger. He's wielding a letter opener," Wolflock called back to Mothy and Dr Qwan, who hadn't pressed forward.

Upon hearing that, the doctor stepped up to the mayor and Mothy joined Wolflock, watching behind them for any intruders or accomplices of the Mayor's.

Wolflock drew out his magnifying glass, keeping his mouth covered with his hand. The worst of the smell was coming from the merman himself. He tried to breathe easily, but the putrid scent of decay made his gut quiver, ready to empty what little food he'd eaten earlier that day.

"What happened, Herfed?" Dr Qwan breathed, his dark eyes wide in alarm.

Wolflock stopped and stared as he addressed the mayor with such seriousness. The doctor glanced at some dim embers under a little iron cauldron and snatched them up, pouring out the flecks of herbal medicines he'd provided the mayor.

"I was just trying to help," Mayor Merlai blubbered. "I thought the medicine would make him better, but he wouldn't go back in the water. Mermaids need to be in the water. They suffocate if they're out for too long."

Wolflock didn't doubt it. The merman was enormous. His head was the size of a cow's, and he could see that Himi had only lasted out of the water for as long as she did because she was so young. The sheer amount of blubber on the merman was enough to crush five adult humans.

"You... They aren't human, Herfed! You can't give them human medicine! I thought you were looking after a diver! A fisher!" Dr Qwan's hands shook so hard that the remains of any sticks or leaves showered back to the ground.

Wolflock ignored Dr Qwan hitting boiling point as he examined the merman's long claws and skin. Mothy, on the other hand, kept his eyes and ears trained on the two adults, ready to intervene.

"Why didn't you bring this to me? Why didn't you tell me?"

Mayor Merlai burst into gasping tears, hiding his face in his hands. "I-I-"

He continued to wail as Wolflock touched the merman's puffy arm. He looked bigger than the ones that approached the ship at Sinalta. As he pushed the icy cold flesh, it felt hard, like a balloon ready to burst. The dark, grey, mottled skin stretched so tightly over the enormous body that he could see the bluish skin in patches between the fur. A deep, blue tone had formed where his body pressed on the cave stones. Sores as big as fingerprints covered the merman's body, and the skin sagged like a wet cloth from his arms and tail. Even his chubby face looked sunken around the cheeks and eyes.

"He came out of the bay..." Wolflock's eyes scanned

over a dark pool of brown liquid. The way the water lapped back and forth, he could tell it led back to the bay. He moved closer to investigate if he could see sunlight from the bay through the water and nearly slipped in the brown slime crawling into the cave.

He moved back to the merman's face, looking at the nose and mouth. A watery brown fluid leaked out in a thin trickle.

"I tried so hard to get him to go back into the water, but he refused, so I brought him fish. I tried so hard to get him back to his pod. I thought if I could keep him alive til the Pisces Moon festival, then he'd just rejoin his family, but he just wouldn't go!" Mayor Merlai's sobs echoed through the cave.

Dr Qwan picked up one of the half-eaten fish, squeezing brown sludge out of it. "This is infected! All the fish are infected! You fed him infected fish, Herfed! Then you gave them the wrong medicine! *Nǐshǎ dé gēn zhū yàng!*" the doctor swore in Xiayahn.

"I didn't know what else to do-hoo-hoo-hoo." Merlai fell back to the ground and splashed in the brown slime, breaking into another coughing fit.

"Lockie?" Mothy patted Dr Qwan on the shoulder. The doctor wiped his eyes.

"I can't believe I wasn't more careful. I vowed to do

no harm. My medicines have killed a being..."

Wolflock used the handle of his magnifying glass to open the merman's mouth, only to see thick brown fluid pooling in the back of his throat.

"No. No, they haven't," Wolflock snarled.

The three of them turned to him as he clenched his fists, glaring hot daggers at the mayor.

"He came into the cave because the brown murk disoriented him in the bay. The disease attacked his skin and throat, probably his gut, too, since he's lost weight rapidly, as you can see from his loose skin. How long has he been dead for, Merlai?"

"You... You see, I tried my-"

"YOUR BEST DOESN'T MATTER WHEN LIVES ARE AT STAKE! HOW LONG HAS HE BEEN DEAD FOR?" Wolflock roared.

He had to protect Himi. One of his few friends was in a danger he couldn't warn them about, and he had to do everything within his power to stop her ending up like this merman. Dying alone, frightened, hungry, and diseased. Confused in a dark place with water he couldn't get back into because of how badly it affected him.

He would crash every ship and tear out every tree to block the bay to save her.

"Two days. He-he's been dead for two days. I

thought he was hibernating... but he's been gone... I just didn't... I couldn't..."

"The brown murk in the bay may make humans cough and lethargic, but in two days, it has caused more rapid decomposition in this mermaid than it should have in a week. Then you fed him infected fish, spreading the disease further. Not only has your incompetence in leading an investigation to find the source of the infection left the bay inhabitable for fish to feed your people, but now it's killed an innocent merman. Great leadership." Wolflock clapped his hands slowly, a livid sneer contorting his jagged features.

Mayor Merlai stopped crying, staring open-mouthed at Wolflock, hiccupping back another coughing fit.

"And why is the town suffering? Because Vanmoinen took terrible business advice from Lord Therym and housed both a toxic brewery set up and slavers. The whole thing exploded, dammed the river, and flushed the murk into the bay where the currents keep it trapped. It started making people sick, and killing aquatic life. All the while, you're just trying to hide the fact that you've been told not to investigate any further and make your Guard gather water to keep the town alive because you don't have enough of a backbone to stand up against the people that prop you up in your cushy minister's chair!"

Wolflock hissed in a low tone that cut through the cavern. Mothy's face had gone pale, his blue eyes wide as they stared at his friend, and Dr Qwan had stepped between the mayor and the sleuth.

"I despise politicians like you. You put your position above what is right."

"Slavers?" Mothy whimpered.

Wolflock's gut plummeted. He realised he hadn't told Mothy what he'd seen at the warehouse. He'd wanted to protect his friend, and, yet, he'd just thrown it out in a wave of vitriol.

"Mothy," he reached out to his friend, who flinched. "I was going to tell you, I just-"

Before he could say another word, he felt a blast from behind him where the merman laid. Wolflock tensed as an explosive wave of brown and blue hurtled his body forward. He hit the stone floor hard as it showered the other three in chunks of merman and brown slime.

Wolflock spat blood and muck from his mouth, gingerly getting to his feet. He wiped as much of the brown slime off as he could, but it clung to him like glue.

"What happened? He just... he just..." Mayor Merlai stammered.

"I think the technical term for what just happened, my good Mayor Herfed Merlai, is Kablooie," Dr Qwan responded in a very matter-of-fact way.

"Mothy, I'm sorry. I got so caught up in everything. I was going to tell you, but there just didn't seem to be a right time."

"It's fine." Mothy grumbled, pulling long strings of slime from his hair. "I mean, it's all fine. I'm sure you would have told me, eventually."

Something about Mothy's tone and the fact that he was still touching his hair put a stone of guilt and doubt in Wolflock's gut.

"Quickly, now." Dr Qwan ushered them back up the tunnel. "We'll wash you off in the top pool. It's still clean. We can't be washing you in bay water."

The doctor looked alarmingly pristine. His white coat didn't have a skerrick of brown slime or merman guts on it. In the light of the colourless flame, he could just make out a silvery shimmer to the doctor's coat.

Is it enchanted? Or made of some exotic grime repellent fibre?

The four of them slipped and slid back up the tunnel to the green pool.

"Is it safe to go into this water?" Mayor Merlai asked, giving a concerned cough.

"Hmm... Let me check," Dr Qwan contemplated the water for a moment before pushing the mayor in with a tremendous splash. The barrel-waisted man bobbed back to the surface, splashing and swimming back to the edge, wiping his face and hair as he approached.

Wolflock snorted as Mothy bouldered into the water, clutching his knees to his chest.

"You too, Mr Felen. In you go," Dr Qwan smirked, snatching the grey match off him as he pushed Wolflock in as well.

He hit the water and completely submerged, keeping his eyes open so he could wipe the brown muck off. The light from the match outside the water lit up just enough for him to see the brown dissolve the moment it touched the water.

Was it the green mineral?

He stared in amazement at his arms as the water cleansed him entirely. Wolflock kicked his feet in the deep pool and broke the surface, paddling back to the others on the edge of the pool. He turned to see Mothy flick water deliberately up at the opening above them, letting it glint in the afternoon sunlight.

"Did you see that? What incredible powers this pool has," Wolflock gurgled as fresh water caught him in the mouth. It had an odd mineral taste to it.

"What do you mean?" Mothy splashed him.

"Well, for starters, it's surprisingly warm. Especially

given the climate and weather. And, secondly, did you see how it dissipated all the brown slime?"

"Oh, that's normal, I suppose. The river did it for you earlier, remember?"

"What?"

Mothy paddled after him back to the edge, and they hopped up on the edge of the pool, wringing out their hair and shirts.

"Aye. When you got covered in the beer sludge at the warehouse and Dr Qwan pushed you into the water, it all disappeared there, too."

"A lot faster, in fact," Dr Qwan drew a small towel from his coat and handed it to Mothy.

Wolflock blinked a few times and stared into the pool, struck deep in thought. What similarities could the river and the rock pool have? They had completely unique elements and minerals inside them. One was from rainwater and the other from distant streams.

Glittering ripples in the water brought his mind to his web of clues as he tried to pull the strands to make sense of the pieces before him. The lumber mill, the mine, the bay. Carpenter, brickmaker, mayor and lord... And their children...

He knew how the bay became infected.

The same brown slime originated from the destroyed

shed at Vanmoinen's property, clearly a result of the brewery explosion, mixed with diseased slaves and human waste. That infected the river in large enough quantities, while also damming the river enough to prevent it from being washed away. This, coupled with the sea currents, meant that the infection remained lodged in the bay.

The fiends had fled with a smaller carriage pulled by a strange, pointed hoofed beast, taking whatever bodies with them they could. Vanmoinen knew about this. He knew about the river and the disease. Wolflock had seen their footprints and Vanmoinen had confessed.

The trail led back to Lord Therym recommending them in the first place, as well as being Vanmoinen's keenest customer. He had also made the nefarious storage renters leave sooner than they intended.

Did that rush to depart cause the mistake that blew up the shed? Wolflock thought as he took off his shoe and wrung out his sock.

The Lord had used the storage facilities to move his mining supplies and goods until all his staff had left because of terrible conditions, which was why Jaxarna had refused to sell her mine to him. Even after her injury with the tunnel collapse. She had integrity when it came to taking ores from the ground and she knew he didn't.

She was so delicate with her processes that she even

used scrying magic to find her ores. Someone who was not as delicate had come through and used a silvery metal implement to find their own samples behind the bubbly stone, though.

Who had been searching through Jaxarna's mine? Lord Therym, his son Najord and Vanmoinen's son had all been there at one stage or another, and all of them had a motive to sabotage Jaxarna's success.

Najord and Therym because she'd recently broken off Girid's engagement now that they would be financially stable without outside assistance.

Had one of them damaged the poorly built brace enough to make it collapse on her? How could they clean the entire bay in four hours? How could they save Himi and her pod?

Wolflock didn't realise they had walked out of the tunnel until the sunlight flashed in front of his eyes. He knew his web had all the threads; he just didn't know how to tie the last few together.

"I would appreciate it," Mayor Merlai began talking as they trekked down the grassy path back to town, "if you all wouldn't mention this to anyone. I don't think it's of consequence, to be frank, but I want you to know that I will do everything in my power to clear the water as quickly as I can."

Wolflock eyed him suspiciously, hearing that his voice was far more melodic than before they'd been swimming. He hadn't coughed once on the way back down.

Mothy and Dr Qwan both raised eyebrows at Wolflock.

"Huh? Oh. Oh yes, that isn't happening."

Mayor Merlai's face dropped.

"If my mermaid friend gets even a sniffle from being in this bay, there will be no dark secret this town holds that I won't spread far and wide. It won't just be you, Merlai. It will be every single sentient being, human, cat, dog, and horse. No secret worm will stay beneath their putrid rock."

"Present company excluded?" Dr Qwan asked with a façade of meekness.

"I suppose you've done your best to avert disaster. You and your wife may be off the hook."

The mayor gulped.

The four of them made their way to the edge of town, seeing a collection of six Guards in their royal blue uniforms dragging someone from their front door.

"What on Pelaia-?" Wolflock exclaimed, jogging up to the scene.

Jaxarna struggled against two Guard grasping her powerful arms and moving her into a large carriage as she wheezed protestations, covering the Guard in dust from the mine. Another two held back Girid, who stood with eyes wide and pale like a ghost. Another stood by soberly observing the situation. Wolflock recognised him. It was Jaimeron.

"What's the meaning of this?" the dark-haired boy snapped.

"Off with you, lad. Nothing to see here."

"What's going on?" Mayor Merlai caught up, panting.

"Oh. Well, we found the culprit, mayor. We've just been provided evidence that Jaxarna has intentionally poisoned the bay and destroyed the lumber mill to gain a monopoly over the town."

"What are you talking about?" Wolflock glared wildly around, his web of clues being torn in the winds of calamity.

"This letter-"

Jaimeron pulled out a pristine envelope that Wolflock snatched away. The Guard went to grab it back, but Mayor Merlai stopped him.

My dear Therym,

I must thank you for your continued assistance in all of my business dealings and apologise again for the inconvenience the separation from my daughter may have caused your son. As I wanted to mention, I have an important business deal I'd like to propose and, as evidence to the success of this, I want to relay the action I have already taken.

As you and I both know, Van's land is on multitudes of ores and mineral deposits, but the fool only ever plants his trees. You and I could make hundreds of thousands of deimas were we to dig it up. I have found a way to leech malachite poisoning into the bay and, since I destroyed the storage shed by the river in Vanmoinen's, everyone will think it's because of his folly. The fool is too proud to say his shed was ruined, and so has everyone thinking the gods are displeased with him and have cut off the river. Once he is banished, we will be able to take the land for a pittance.

Please maintain the utmost secrecy in this matter as it could put us both at stake.

Your friend always,

Jaxarna

Wolflock pressed his lips so tightly they went white as he read the damning letter. "And... who gave you this?"

Jaimeron's shoulders squared, and he looked over at the crying mother and child.

"I don't know why, but that came from Girid herself."

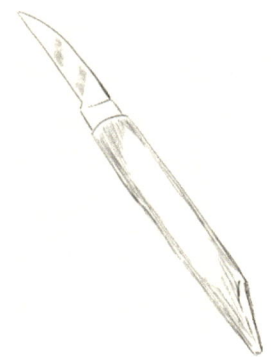

CHAPTER 9

Shades of Poison

They could do nothing as they carted away Jaxarna with the Guard. Wolflock's mind flared as he took in the scene. It seared itself into his brain. He knew it was wrong. It was so wrong. Jaxarna was innocent. This letter was a complete lie, and, yet, here it was. Mothy moved to Girid and touched her arm, trying to comfort the shocked girl along with the mayor. Dr Qwan peered over Wolflock's shoulder at the note with a stern face.

"Jaxa wrote this?"

"Supposedly." Wolflock dug in his pockets for the letters he'd taken from Lord Therym's office.

"Something looks off about it. She has sent me letters before. Notes, packages, requests for pain herbs. This looks... not like her." Dr Qwan put his finger to his nose as he pondered the note.

Wolflock compared Jaxarna's letter to the recent note. The first thing he noticed was that the handwriting was very similar, but not the same. Jaxarna's older letter was rough and heavy, sloping right. The ink on both pages was smudged in only the way a left-handed person caused. Wolflock had plenty of experience with his writing hand being blackened and perfect handwriting being unceremoniously splodged as he learned to write faster.

"Jaxarna is left-handed?" he asked the doctor.

"When it isn't injured, she is. Yes."

The other note also sloped right, but it was far lighter. It could have been her mood when writing it, but it was more likely that a softer hand had written this second note. Next was the paper and ink. Jaxarna's old note was thoroughly speckled in dried clay and dirt. This recent note was pristine. Jaxarna had been very dusty as the Guard escorted her away. There was no way she could have written this note and kept the paper so clean. But who had written it? Who had framed her, and why had Girid been the deliverer of such damning work?

"This is my fault," Dr Qwan whispered, his dark eyebrows pinching in a frown. "If I hadn't told her to go home, she would have been able to hide in the mines. She wouldn't be blamed for this letter."

"My good doctor," Wolflock interjected, "she may be far worse off continuing to work in her condition than being locked up for a few hours. Neither of us believe Jaxarna wrote this letter, but the culprit has given us more than one clue to find out who they are."

"What makes you say that?"

"I believe that this letter not only shows us who tried to drive Jaxarna out of her mine, but also who poisoned the bay."

"Poisoned the bay? But wasn't it an accident? Caused by the poor brewing techniques of the..." Dr Qwan lowered his voice as he spied Mothy, "...slavers?"

"That's what I thought too, but this paper has an odd dust on it, wouldn't you say?"

Wolflock held it up to the doctor's face, and he sneezed loudly, blowing tiny purple particles off it.

"Mmm... Oh my... Yes..." Dr Qwan's eyes dilated, and a dopey grin crossed his face.

"Are you well, doctor?" Wolflock frowned.

"Mmm... Yes... I think I may need a little sit for a moment."

Wolflock took his arm and led him to Mothy and Girid, who looked similarly dopey with her pupils wide.

"She's not well, Lockie." Mothy bit his lip in concern.

"Neither is the doctor. Let's go inside and get something for them to drink. Maybe that will help."

The front door to the little house flapped in the breeze, banging against the perfect brickwork. Directly down the main hallway, they found the kitchen and sat the two dizzy people down on sweetly carved little stools. Tears leaked down Girid's cheeks as her pupils pulsed, slowly shrinking back to normal in waves.

Wolflock scrutinised her face and then turned to Dr Qwan. He had a theory. A purple glowing thread in his web of clues.

"Doctor, stand up."

Dr Qwan didn't hesitate. He shot up to his feet.

"Doctor, sit down."

He sat down again.,

"Doctor, withdraw a pen and paper from your pockets."

Without question, he drew out a notebook, wooden pen, and square ink bottle.

"Write exactly what I say."

"What are you doing?" Mothy asked, wiping

Girid's tears from her face.

Wolflock gave Mothy a look that said he was being very serious. "I, Dr Qwan Loong hereby announce that I am a chicken and shall only treat poultry in my practise. I also renounce my eternal match to Mr Wolflock F. Felen as he is a far more superior mind to myself."

"Yes, Mr... Wolflock... F... Felen..." Dr Qwan slurred, scratching the message down.

Before he could sign, Wolflock snatched the notebook away, letting the doctor finish his scratching on the smooth wood.

"Doctor? Are you aware of what you've written?"

Dr Qwan hummed with a blank smile on his face but seemed pleasantly oblivious.

"Mothy, get them some water."

Mothy hesitated as if he was waiting for Wolflock to use his manners, but let it slide as the situation was more dire than the necessary proper conduct. He clattered in the kitchen until he found a pair of wooden goblets. With a few pumps from the long handle at the stone sink, they filled with clean, clear water. As Mothy helped Girid take a few sips, Wolflock threw the cup of water into Dr Qwan's face.

"Ah!" the doctor spluttered. "A shower? Lovely. I thought I was getting a bit pongy too."

Mothy couldn't help but chuckle, but Wolflock's face remained frozen.

"Doctor. Are you aware of what you just did?"

Dr Qwan wrung out his long ponytail as he thought. Wolflock noted that the water beaded off his coat in a most peculiar fashion.

"I did something just now? I recall... Now, correct me if this is wrong, but sniffing a letter?"

"So you don't remember writing this?" Wolflock thrust the newly written note in front of him.

Dr Qwan stared at the note and began laughing. "I suppose I need to brush up on my chicken speak! No, my good lad. I didn't write this. You really like that match, don't you? Wonderful penmanship. It looks just like my handwriting and everything."

Wolflock caught Mothy's eye with a knowing stare. "Doctor... Could that purple powder-"

"The Dominia Mendis Impertio particles?"

"Yes. You called it Lady Mind Master earlier. Could that induce amnesia as well as the suggestibility you mentioned?"

"Well, yes, but it would have to be in a highly concentrated dose. Not the stuff we found at the destroyed shed."

Wolflock placed the fake letter from Jaxarna on

the table and moved to Girid, drawing out his magnifying glass as he analysed her face. It was clean. Too clean.

"This will be a little... unsavoury. Doctor, do you have any pepper in those pockets?" Wolflock drew out his handkerchief and tipped Girid's head back. Mothy held her shoulders for support, looking weary of Wolflock's actions.

"Let me see... Ah! There we have it. Pepper? What for?"

Wolflock took the little jar of fine grey powder, took a pinch in his fingers, and while holding the cloth in front of Girid's face, flicked the pepper right up her nose. She coughed and sneezed into the handkerchief three times before her eyes watered and her eyes returned to their normal size.

"What happened?" She sniffed. Wolflock took the cloth from her and put it in front of the doctor.

"Ah. Snot. Just what I needed to help Jaxa." Dr Qwan rolled his eyes.

"Use your scope to see if there are particles in her mucus," Wolflock urged.

"Why does ma need help?"

"Where were you before you came home?" Wolflock pushed.

"I went..."

Before she could answer, a hulking figure threw open the back door and rushed to her. It was Vanmoinen's son. "Girid? Girid! What's going on?"

The handsome blond man stood taller than anyone in the room, with strands of straight hair coming free from his small, high ponytail. Girid blushed and tried to push his hands below the table, but he took hers, shaking. "What are they doing here?"

"Hase, shh... These are my friends."

"They tried to dig up dirt around the lumber mill," the young man protested, staying tight to Girid's side.

"They can't find secrets where there are none, Hase. They're here to help."

"How?"

"Enough of this. Girid, where were you before you gave the authorities the letter that has sent your mother to the Guard tower!" Wolflock snapped.

"I... what?" Her hazel eyes brimmed with tears.

"That's why I came here. As soon as I heard, I knew something was wrong. You'd never do something like that," the carpenter's son said firmly.

"I don't expect you to remember having written the letter, but it's not in your mother's handwriting. It's in yours. You're very similar, but you're not left-handed. This paper is also clean. Nothing your mother touches stays this clean. There were particles of a powder I believe to have influenced your behaviour, but I need you to tell me where you have been, so I know where this came from. That will tell us who is responsible for framing your mother."

Girid flushed scarlet. "I... I went to Najord's house."

Hase paled and let go of her hands. "I thought we were done with that."

"I went to return his music to him. I didn't think it was right for me to use his songs since we're not... well... I wanted to do the right thing. All I remember is returning them and then waking up in my kitchen."

Wolflock saw Hase's huge shoulders relax. "So you were at Lord Therym's house. That's it, then. Now, I need to figure out how to reveal him."

"What?" Mothy gasped, "You know who has done all this?"

"I have a fairly clear idea. There are a few missing pieces, but, to reveal them, we have to get the perpetrator to come out of their web of lies. I need them to write something to us without thinking, though."

"What do you mean?"

"The key to finding out who used the Lady Mind Master powder on Girid to send her mother to the guard tower used a specific type of paper. I need them to use it again. We need something to rush them, but also not alert them to what they're doing."

"Well, they can't write it to you. They'd have to write it to Girid, wouldn't they? Maybe something about her needing help."

"Hmm... needing help, you say? What if it was giving her help in return for the thing they're after?"

"And what's that?" Hase and Mothy asked in unison.

Girid sighed. "The mine."

Everyone turned to watch her reaction, but Wolflock nodded. "Yes. That's what all this has been about, hasn't it? Vanmoinen was jealous of your mother's good fortune. It gave you both the freedom to cut off your ties to Therym and Najord." As he spoke, Wolflock noticed Hase clench his fists on the table at the mention of Najord. "And, with the proximity so close to the bay, it was easy to blame any infection on the activity that went on in there."

"So we use the mine as bait?"

"Exactly. I need you to write a letter we will send to Therym and Vanmoinen."

"Why my father?"

"Because we need to make it believable that Girid

is desperate." Wolflock rolled his eyes. "We'll tell them you think the mine is cursed and that you want to be rid of it. You're going to ask them for the better offer written as quickly as you can."

"But any sale will leave us destitute. They'll see through it. Especially Therym. He may have terrible mining practises, but he's an astute businessman. He'll know it's a lie."

Wolflock pinched his chin between his thumb and index knuckle, pacing in the small kitchen. "Ahah! Tell them they also need to write you a poem for you to sing this evening. A noble family in Mystentine has requested you to make your debut as a professional singer at their next ball and it will begin your dream career. Tell them to meet us at the entrance of the mine."

Girid blushed with a bittersweet smile. Wolflock's words evidently made her excited that one day they could be real, but also sad that she had to lie about them now. Hase beamed at her before standing up to find paper for her to pen her note on. After a few minutes, they had a fully formulated lie, requesting both men to meet at the mine with the mayor to officiate the transaction.

"Now we head over?" Hase asked.

"We have to get Jaxarna, first." Wolflock nodded.

"And you have to write your poem, too. Otherwise

it's really not believable." Mothy grinned and pushed the paper and pen to the blushing Hase.

CHAPTER 10

Taste of Their Own Medicine

Wolflock paced back and forth in the afternoon sun outside of Jaxarna's mine, pinching his chin as he prepared for Therym's arrival. He knew that his entire web pointed directly at the Lord. All his evidence said that the nobleman had manipulated the mayor, the carpenter, and the brickmaker with subversive influences, but he didn't have the final information to tie his web around the fiend. So he paced.

Mothy tried to distract Girid by asking her to teach

him how to sing, but he sounded so awful they had to stop after an hour of screeching. Dr Qwan fiddled with his experiments, measuring powders and liquids to get the water samples to respond accurately. At one point, a live duck flapped out of his coat and across the hills away from them. They all just stopped and stared, then returned to their pensiveness.

The sun sat barely an hour above the horizon when Mayor Merlai, Jaimeron and his Guard troop arrived. The mayor tried to approach Wolflock and ask him what was going on, but the teenager just held up his hand for quiet and continued pacing.

Half an hour later, Therym, Njord, Vanmoinen and Hase all arrived, poems in hand, looking apprehensive of each other. Mothy collected the poems and brought them to Girid, who nodded thoughtfully. Wolflock watched all of their postures and gestures before moving to look over Girid's shoulder.

Hase looked nervous, but in a bashful sense. It was obvious why. Vanmoinen's eyes rolled in contempt at being so close to the mine, and he muttered about the request being stupid. Wolflock could sense mountains of jealousy and contempt for the situation. Najord looked as bored as ever, and Lord Therym looked like Yule had come early. His face was lit up with glee and he talked to everyone around him as if they were old friends, uncaring that the livelihoods of two women were at stake.

"So, how quickly are we going about all this?" Lord Therym grinned.

"Once Girid has decided, we'll have the paperwork signed and ready here." Mayor Merlai showed him the papers with a stiff, half smile.

Girid turned to Wolflock, her hands shaking. "What do you think?"

He took up the four papers and analysed them alongside Jaxarna's fake note. Hase's had been written with Dr Qwan's paper and ink in Jaxarna's house, and so was lightly tainted with clay dust and dirt. His handwriting scratched the page with stiff, large strokes, but remained light, as if he was unsure of himself. The twenty lined poem had blemishes where he had scored out wrong words and rewritten them around the black marks. Each line was filled with childish love and adoration with a basic rhyme that would have been a tavern or inn favourite, but no one of any intellect.

Vanmoinen's torn notebook page came from the back of some kind of pre-lined margins ledger and was lazily scrawled in handwriting similar to that as the map at his lumber mill. It was only a five lined limerick with the lines drawn so hard they left firm imprints on the other side of the page.

Lord Therym's was on exquisite paper with delicate green painted plants in the top left and bottom right corners. The eight lines of his poem looked stiff, as if he'd found a love poem in a book and copied it, emphasised by the lighter, unsure pen strokes.

It struck Wolflock that this wasn't a match for any of the details he'd been looking for.

This wasn't the shiny paper with the borders that soaked through to the underside. There were no traces of purple despite being right next to the plant he suspected had been used on Girid.

"Lord Therym," Wolflock spoke in a firm tone.

Clearly everyone had taken it as the announcement as two of the Guards stepped up to his side, ready to seize him. Hase's face dropped in shock and Wolflock realised he'd forgotten why they were there. Hase thought this was really a competition to see who would marry Girid. The fool.

Lord Therym bounced like a child on the balls of his feet, but stopped as Wolflock shook his head. "How old is the plant on your desk?"

His smile faltered. "It... It's only just getting its first flowers, so I'd say six months. How did you know about-"

"Have you prepared any tonics or powders from it?"

"N-no. It's purely decorative."

Wolflock's eyes narrowed as he looked over at the lying lord. He had already gotten the bags for the seeds and flowers wrong, as he'd heard in the conversation from Therym's office. He couldn't read the instructions on the pot, so he was likely to get it wrong again without guided instruction. He lied about it being decorative, but there was a note of truth to what he said about preparing powders from it. The more Wolflock thought about it, the less it seemed that the plant was intended as a gift for the lord in the first place. Had it been given to Therym to mask who it was truly intended for?

He glanced at Najord's, thinking he would have to continue his analysis of Therym's poem and needing to refresh his eyes on a new piece, when he saw a familiar style of black border. It soaked through to the opposite side. As he flipped it over to check, it wasn't the match of paper that caught his eye as much as it was the purple dust stuck to it.

Remembering some of the music paper he had collected from the destroyed storage shed, Wolflock drew out the largest piece he had wedged between the pages of his journal. The borders matched. His eyes moved to Najord, who leaned against the wall of the mine, cleaning his pen with his silver penknife. Wolflock's brain buzzed as the threads of clues knotted before his very eyes. Najord returned his knife into his pocket, but, in order to do so, he had to lift his baggy shirt. Attached to his belt next to his pocket was a small purple bag.

Wolflock felt as if his guts had turned to ice. Najord was the son of a wealthy nobleman, just like he was. He resented his father, just like Wolflock did. They both loved music. The similarities mounted in his mind, and he felt disgusted by them.

"It's Najord," he breathed, feeling the lines of his web shine brightly as it all fell into place. With each clue, it all became clear.

Mayor Merlai nodded reluctantly, and the Guards stepped up to Najord, seizing his arms.

"What? What is the meaning of this?" he barked with surprising energy.

"Unhand him! What on Pelaia are you thinking!?" Lord Therym snapped.

"I'm sorry, Therym. Your son is being charged with contaminating the bay, forgery, coercion and blackmail," Jaimeron responded.

"And you can add attempted murder of Jaxarna,

and the incidental murder of a mermaid to that," Wolflock added.

"You have no proof!" Lord Therym roared as Najord tried to yank his arms free.

"Mr Wolflock Felen? Are you sure?" asked Mayor Merlai in his simpering tone.

Wolflock's mind flashed hot at the mayor's tone. In that instant, he knew in no uncertain terms this weak politician was going to let someone off because of their position if he didn't display everything he knew. Just like what had happened in Plugh.

He wouldn't stand for it.

In that moment, Wolflock felt himself tear away from everything that resembled boys like Najord. He may understand him, but he had vowed to never be like him. He would sooner do away with his title and power than let justice go unserved by it.

"Yes. Without the shadow of a doubt. And I have all the proof any of you will need right here in my hand, and in this mine." He waved the sheets of paper in the orange sunlight. "These papers have a particular sheen to them, and you'll often find that that uniqueness is the first thing that eliminates clandestinity. The border that soaks through to the underside and the pre-lined musical bars show this paper is in easy reach of the writer, as though they use it often and, subsequently, their love to use it while composing. This is what you had Girid write the false note from Jaxarna on. This is what we found in the wreckage of the storage shed, and this is what you have written some of your best poetry on in order to win a mine you didn't even want. My question is, why? Najord, why?"

The young man's pale face contorted with rage, transforming his features into something monstrous. Wolflock looked at Girid, whose expression was one of pure revulsion.

"You can't prove that at all!"

"Sorry, that was rhetorical. I know why you did it, but we'll get to that in a moment. But, tell me this: were you hoping to destroy your father, or did you just not care if you did?"

Najord thrashed about, refusing to answer.

"N-Najord? What is he saying?" Therym paled.

"He's lying. He's an outsider coming in to stir trouble, that's all. There's nothing he can say that would prove anything." Najord stopped, his eyes going wide with a false epiphany. Wolflock could see his mouth twitch with a contemptuous smirk. "Unless he planted this evidence he's been talking about in your office, father."

"What?"

"I saw him in there earlier! He was rifling through your papers. I thought he was an assistant of yours for the festival. He must have been planting evidence to frame me!"

All eyes turned to the black-haired boy as rage bubbled up inside him. He thought he had seen himself in Najord. Bored with life, disdainful of those less brilliant than himself, and desperate to get out of his family's shadow. But no. Najord was just a lying, spoiled brat who would use any trick to reach his means.

Well, I can play that game, too, he thought darkly.

Wolflock saw the sun touch the horizon, and knew he didn't have long. When the sun went down and the moon came out, the mermaids would come to the bay. They had to have their solution now or else Himi would die.

He could see her happy and smiling face leaping from wave to wave, surrounded by her loved ones, playfully rushing the fish to their favourite destination. Then, without fear or hesitation, swimming right into the murk of the bay, coughing, choking, and leaving, not knowing why anything had changed. Being powerless to help and naïve as to why her pod was dying.

Wolflock eyed the purple bag at Najord's side. He would get justice for Himi, Jaxarna and Vanmoinen. He

213

wouldn't let a corrupt family have exorbitant power over the town.

"I believe a demonstration of your intent is in order." He tugged Najord's purple bag free and felt the inner lining of stones grind together. "Did you think you'd be needing this?"

The young noble's eyes went wide with fear. "Don't! That's my only-"

"This is what he did to Girid earlier today, forcing her to write a letter on his paper, as if her mother was asking for help to take over Vanmoinen's lumber mill. All to destroy their mining project." Wolflock tipped the bag entirely into his hand and blew it into Najord's face, making him cough and splutter. As the young man's eyes dilated, Wolflock turned the bag inside out to make sure he had eliminated all of it.

"Release him," Wolflock instructed the Guards. They looked to Jaimeron, who nodded, his burly arms crossed in front of his armour.

Najord's shoulders drooped, and a goofy grin spread across his face. Everyone else remained silent. Lord Therym had gone so pale he looked as if he might faint.

"Najord, can you hear me?" Wolflock asked.

"Mmm.... Ja."

"I need you to answer my questions honestly. Can you do that?"

"Ja..."

"How did you find out there was malachite in this copper mine?"

"I scratched it with my knife when father and I went to talk with them in the mine. I got bored waiting for father to plead for the engagement to be kept."

"Why?"

"So he could get the mine when we were married."

"Did your father know about the malachite?"

"He knew before I did. I just found out how much of it was in here. I came back here every night for the past fortnight."

"And you were dressed as Hase?"

"Ja..."

"In order to make Jaxarna believe Hase was trying to sabotage the mine, yes?"

"Mmm... Ja." Najord's eyes glazed over as Wolflock said the bricklayer's name.

"What?" Girid's eyes went wide. "Why? How? Your father would never let you go out dressed like my Hase."

"I snuck out after dark. I stole his clothes."

"You stole my clothes?" Hase leapt to his feet.

"I followed her," he slumped his head towards Girid, "and found her sharing my music with you in the forest. I stole your clothes after you finished taking them off. I was looking for my songs but took the lot instead."

Hase and Girid went beetroot red.

"When was this?" Wolflock interrupted before Vanmoinen could reprimand his son's deceit.

"The day after the bricklayer bought the mine and broke off the engagement. I had only shared my music with her," he nodded at Girid again, "with the knowledge that my intellectual property would be safe under the contract of our marriage... my mistake..."

Even with that sleepy grin, venom laced his tone.

"And when did you find the storage shed of illegal brewing materials and slaves?" Wolflock gazed around at the faces of the onlookers for their responses. Universal shock rippled across them, including Lord Therym. Vanmoinen squirmed in shame.

"I knew the whole time. I'm the one who made sure my father approached the lumberjack about using his empty sheds for storage."

"With your powder?"

"Ja..."

Lord Therym jerked back in horror, shaking his head at the information.

"And how did you know the sheds were empty?"

"She," he nodded to Girid, "would go down there and sing. I followed her. Then he," he nodded to Hase, "joined her with his lute and ruined it. I had to make sure she sang my songs right... They aren't made for a lute."

"So, you were at the lumber storage sheds the day one was destroyed?"

"Ja..."

"How was it destroyed?"

"I... knocked out a leg of one of the big brewing pots. It crashed into the other one and everything caught on fire."

"Why were you in there?"

"To... stop the escaping slave. They'd seen my face a few times. They were going to give me away."

"That's why you were there when it exploded?"

"No..."

"Then why?"

"To get more powder. Astraxis had promised me more, but his men wouldn't cough up. I was nearly out... I am out now..." he looked mournfully at the purple sprinkled over the dirt path.

"Did you push the debris into the river, or did it just fall that way?"

"I didn't push it into the river like that..." Therym

sighed with relief as Najord spoke, but a sinister smile crawled across that dozy face. "But I'm glad it did. My father is ruined for keeping me under his thumb. Astraxis is ruined because he wouldn't give me more powder. She's ruined for stealing my songs. And the lumberjack and his son are ruined for being stupid."

Lord Therym shook his head in devastated disappointment, but the rest of the room glared at Najord with a terrible fury for his disdain for the people he knew.

"I found the same music paper with this silky sheen in Najord's hands at Lord Therym's house, as well as scraps of it at the destroyed storage shed, and finally," Wolflock waved the fake Jaxarna letter, "this one incriminating Jaxarna. We have the same paper here that Najord has presented his poem on in order to win the mine today. Winning this mine would have given him true financial independence for a time, as he could sell the malachite to the magic users in Mystentine, releasing him from his familial duties.

"Everyone thought Jaxarna had started the infection into the bay with her mining, but her practises are so refined and careful that there was no way she could have contaminated it. The tide, also, does not reach high enough inside the caves to touch the malachite crystals. The pool she has been swimming in collects only rainwater. Dr Qwan, what are the common symptoms of malachite poisoning?"

Without missing a beat, Dr Qwan smiled, counting the symptoms off on his fingers, "Shortness of breath, chesty cough, sinus inflammation and general anaemia."

"Thank you, doctor. So, Jaxarna wasn't the first to be infected with what is in the bay. She was the first to suffer from malachite poisoning. I also know that Jaxarna was not the one to write the note here, as everything she touches becomes layered in clay dust from her work as a bricklayer and from the mine. Every seat, every door handle, every tool and, of course, every piece of paper she comes into contact with, becomes stained brown. Similarly with Vanmoinen, everything he touches is sprinkled with wood shavings from his own occupation at the lumber mill.

"Two weeks ago, the illegal brewery exploded with Najord's assistance, covering much of the evidence that slavers were using it, awaiting a Mr Astraxis to collect them. The contaminated beer, mixed with the refuse of diseased people and the newly dammed river, flowed down into the town and into the bay, where it remains because of the ice and currents outside of the bay. Najord then used this catastrophe to fuel the dissent between Jaxarna and the town, positioning his father as the master manipulator. But there were a few details that just didn't add up. One of them being, why would Therym be gifted an immature *Dominia Mendis Impertio*---"

"Also known as Lady Mind Master," Dr Qwan interjected.

"-in a pot with instructions he can't read?"

The surrounding audience remained silent.

"Because it wasn't meant for him. It was meant for someone in the house that could read Shell. Someone who was less in the public eye than Lord Therym. Someone who would go unnoticed and was apathetic enough to reliably use this powder demonstrated here, in this specific purple bag in which Mothy, Dr Qwan and I all heard Mr Astraxis telling Lord Therym to put the flowers into. Blue for seeds, purple for flowers, is that correct?"

His piercing blue eyes cut to Lord Therym, who took a shaking step back as if he were about to run. He looked at his son, who still managed to glare contemptuously back through his dopey grin, and nodded.

"Someone who also knew, if any scientists or mages from Mystentine were to come and offer assistance, that they would be found out. I found the same purple powder on Mayor Merlai's Lucimpus coat in his office. The same coat he came to your office in to discuss how to get assistance from Mystentine. Is it true that, when he was leaving, you ambushed him, using your powder to convince him to stop seeking aid from Mystentine?"

As Wolflock turned his attention to Najord again, the mayor gasped in horror. His eyes were filled with tears.

"Ja... It wasn't the first time, either. I had to use it on him two more times to make sure he only asked for fish from Irid and, then, so he thought he had some silly award to win if he kept his mouth shut. Lot of good that did me."

"Good to know that the powder doesn't completely erase your repugnant personality," Wolflock scoffed. "Things weren't moving fast enough for you, though, were they? If Girid could sing at the festival tonight without giving you recognition, agents from Mystentine would scout her and take all the glory, wouldn't she? That's why, last week, you sabotaged the wooden beams with your silver knife. I found the traces of silver and the cut in the wood. You weakened it enough that it came down on Jaxarna, injuring her chest and exacerbating her lung condition even more. Did you mean to kill or maim her?"

"I did not mean it to get the bricklayer. It was meant to land on her."

Najord nodded again to Girid, who paled. Hase wrapped his arms around the shaking lady, snarling at the noble boy.

"Ma thought your father had sold her bad wood! That's why she's been so spiteful this past week."

Vanmoinen stared in horror. "I... I would never. I could never. I would have rather refused to sell her anything at all rather than have her injured."

Wolflock saw Najord's pupils begin to contract as the powder lessened its grip on him.

"Finally, I know the answer to this, but for the benefit of those present, why did you do all this? To what end?"

Najord huffed out of his nose as fury cut creases into his bored face. "To be free... of my father. Of this town. Of all these idiots. I want to compose the greatest music of all time, and I could never accomplish that in this backwater town with a foolish, unfaithful fiancé. I deserve to have the greatest orchestra at my disposal, and these country bumpkin fools would never give me that. So, I took it. This mine belongs to me. My father's estate is mine. I will have all the money I need to fund my own endeavours, and no one will tell me otherwise."

Wolflock let the vile words spill from his entitled mouth and silence suffocated the air between all of them. He looked at the mayor, who still eyed Lord Therym as if asking for permission to do the right thing. Such a weak-willed politician would never stand up for what was right and, as the sun melted into the watery horizon, he knew he was out of time.

"And so, Captain Jaimeron," Wolflock turned to the leader of the Guard, "I leave this evidence and confession in your capable hands. What punishment will be most suitable? Can I suggest he help lay out some kind of net or device to prevent the mermaids from entering the bay and suffering the same fate as the one the mayor was attempting to care for?"

Jaimeron coughed uncomfortably. "Uh. Well, we'll have a trial first and then he'll likely be put to hard labour until all the families who have suffered feel that they have received recompense. He won't be doing any conducting for a few years with this mess he has to clean up-"

"Clean up!" Dr Qwan shouted, making them all jump. He began flinging things from his jacket pockets as he dug through them. After a few moments, he pulled out his water analysis kit and laid it out before them on the ground. "Excellent. Here we are. And the last ingredient..."

He tapped a fine white powder into each test tube. The first turned black, the second turned cloudy white, the third turned clear, and the fourth-

BANG!

-exploded.

Dr Qwan fell back and Wolflock and Mothy rushed to his aid, helping him sit back up.

"Alright! Don't mix it with pure magnesium. Good to know. I have the answer!" He smiled brightly up at the boys. "Fresh water. The answer has been fresh water all along!"

Wolflock thought back to how Dr Qwan had pushed him into the river and the malachite pond. Both of which had been completely fresh water.

"That's why it's able to thrive in bodies. Humans are full of salt, and mermaids even more so." Dr Qwan said in a matter-of-fact tone.

This is how we'll save Himi, Wolflock thought, filled with determination.

"Jaimeron! Gather your men." He stood up, summoning every inch of authority he could muster. "We need to clear a dam."

CHAPTER 11

Clean Sailing

Jaimeron leaped to action the moment a plan had been decided on. Wolflock couldn't help but see a defiant smirk across his golden bearded face as he neglected to ask the mayor for any kind of permission. He ordered two of his troops to escort Najord to the guardhouse and replace Jaxarna with him in the cell. He then ordered the rest of his Guard to get the strongest, fastest horses available and to meet them on the way to Vanmoinen's collapsed shed.

Wolflock, Mothy, Dr Qwan and the others began their run out of town. As they reached the walls, Wolflock turned to look at the sun for how much time they had left and saw Lord Therym was no longer with them. Scoffing, he hauled himself faster, sprinting along the road to the lumber mill.

The first time it took them over half an hour to reach their destination, but, while speeding forward with dire consequences chasing them, they made it in less than half that time.

They made it to the shed of debris and started wrenching planks of wood free. The chilly afternoon air chilled the sweat that poured off their brows. Wolflock used the same motion he'd learned on the Silver Ice Hair to haul rigging, working feverishly to free the river. Small spouts of clear water soon began trickling through the mess, clearing the brown slime around them.

After just a few minutes, they found that the smaller pieces weren't the problem. One of the back doors with its twisted, metal brackets had lodged itself tightly into the ground and between boulders. Wolflock and Mothy were unafraid of the brown slime, having seen the effects the clean water had on it, and got into the riverbed to dislodge the door. Jaimeron and his Guard tugged from the top, but the piece wouldn't move. Even after attaching Vanmoinen's elk, it wouldn't move.

"It's no good, boys. It's stuck fast. We'll have to

wait for aid. Vanmoinen, get your axes."

Wolflock punched the door as anxiety gripped his throat. Himi might already be in the bay. They didn't have time. Why wouldn't it just move?

The sun vanished and Girid ran about lighting torches she'd found in the wreckage. As the artificial light illuminated the pile of broken and twisted wood, Wolflock only let Mothy see the hot tears burning down his grubby cheeks. Mothy gripped his friend's upper arm, his face quivered as if he was about to start crying too, but he held strong for Wolflock.

"Come on, boys. We did our best. Come find some tools to help." Jaimeron called, offering his hand down to them.

"Not just yet," roared a proud voice from just beyond the first treeline.

A great rumbling of powerful hooves rolled up to them, and Lord Therym sat atop a huge bull on the bank of the river, another following him. The pair were thicker than a carriage and their shining horns curved around their heads like earthy halos. Wolflock had never been happier to see the man.

"Attach these hooks to the base and my boys will pull it free."

"Are you sure?" Mothy called out, but Wolflock

had already done the calculations.

He knew how powerful horses were, and, by the size of those healthy bulls, he had no doubt that they'd tear it free with ease. He latched the two hooks under the door and yanked on them to make sure they were secure.

"I've seen them pull over houses, my boy. This is a walk in the paddock for them!"

The bulls put tension on the ropes, holding them taught until the boys were free of the riverbed. Mothy then leaped forward and grabbed a section of wall, wiggling it free from the remaining rubbish.

"What are you doing? The bulls can take care of this without issue."

Mothy smirked at him through his straining. "Don't you want to see your plan work without delay?"

"Yes? But we'll have to walk... Oh!"

Wolflock realised what his friend meant and jumped forward to help. The rest of the helpers looked in wonder at what they were doing as they held the large section of wall steadily out of the way.

"Bit different from barrels and planks, right?" Mothy chuckled, holding the boards above his head.

"I expect so. Ready?"

"Ready!"

"On three."

The bulls pulled downstream, and the wood groaned and whined. Metal scraped and water gushed.

"One."

A deep cracking in the dam filled them with suspense.

"Two."

The two bulls heaved forward under Lord Therym's command and the dam shattered down the middle as the door splintered into hundreds of pieces. The water rushed through with red and orange seams from the firelight.

"THREE!" Wolflock shouted. The boys leaped into the water after the debris, tucking the piece of wall under their knees.

The rolling torrent of water tumbled the planks of wood and thatch under them, and they rode the wave into the forest. They hadn't anticipated the darkness. The sun had disappeared as the thin canopy of pine trees shaded them from its lingering light. Wolflock sat at the back and helped steer the makeshift raft, following Mothy's movements. They jolted this way and that, trying to keep back far enough to not get sucked under the rapids as they refreshed the river with new life.

Then it got even darker. They hit a thicker part of the wood and desperately tried to stay in the water and attached to their wall.

"I can't see!" Mothy cried out from in front.

"Just hang on!" Wolflock felt his knuckles ache from gripping the plank on either side of him.

Just as he thought they were bound to crash and drown, a greenish blue light glowed under them as the moon swanned out behind the clouds.

"It's the algae! It's in the water." Wolflock called from behind Mothy, who he could now see the silver shape of in front of him.

The rolling waves glittered between the moonlight and the glowing algae, lighting their path all the way through the forest and down through the town. They improved their turning as the river roared through the town, cleaning the slimy canal with ease. People stared and pointed at them as they flashed past on their raft. After what felt like hours, but had only been a few minutes, Wolflock, Mothy, and the river hit the bay.

Their raft rocked front to back as the fast water hit the slow. They both tried to see if their plan had worked and if the bay had been cleansed, but they nearly sent the raft off kilter and fell in. The boys scrambled back onto the wooden platform, laughing as they helped each other on again. People stood all along the shoreline, waiting, whispering to each other as they watched.

Wolflock heard Mothy catch his breath as they watched the water. The force of their trip had sent them into the middle of the bay and the water still looked brown. Wolflock frowned, glancing nervously at the sea to the West.

"So... why are you doing this?" Mothy asked abruptly.

"The town will starve without it," was Wolflock's brief response.

"Uh huh... But why are you doing this? Why do you want to help Creast? What are you getting out of it?"

"Mothy!" Wolflock gasped in mock outrage. "I'll have you know I am very altruistic and that you would think otherwise wounds me!"

Mothy just looked at him with bored eyes, but a telling smirk.

There was a long silence for a moment, and Wolflock looked over the bay.

"Himi is out there... If these mermaids get sick, then she might too. I don't want to risk that when there is something I could do to stop it."

Mothy touched his heart. "Lockie... That's really kind of-"

"Also, this is the biggest port in the Northwest, and it'll be a pain to get back home if it isn't functioning at full

231

capacity. Also," he grinned as Mothy smacked his own forehead, "the Mayor will owe me a favour surely for doing this for him and solving the mystery."

"What am I going to do with you, Lockie?" Mothy sighed.

"Come along on adventures. The mundane would deem it insane to try to keep me out of trouble?" Wolflock shrugged.

"Someone has to." His best friend chuckled, but soon stopped. "Lockie... What if it doesn't work? Was it worth it?"

"Was what worth it? Anything is worth righting a wrong."

"But... What if you did something wrong to reach it?"

"Ends justify means, Mothy. What's all this about?"

Mothy squeezed the water out of his hair and wiped his face, looking away. "The... the purple powder. I've seen similar things used like that before. On slaves. And, you didn't tell me you knew there had been slavers in that shed."

Wolflock's gut twisted. Didn't Mothy understand? He'd used a tool against a bad person. Why was he upset?

"I'd never use it on you. You have to know that." He put his hand on Mothy's wet shirt.

His friend didn't make eye contact with him again. Wolflock went to say something else, but the raft thudded against something and rocked them both.

The moon shone in all its beauty above them, and the water under them glowed. The algae highlighted the edges of the entire bay and as their eyes travelled to the centre; they saw a deep blue light swirling amongst the cleansing wisps of water.

"There's the jewel!" Mothy gasped, pointed so fast Wolflock had to catch him before he fell into the water.

Wolflock smiled as he saw it. The stone was gigantic. A roughly shaped shard of sapphire, polished by centuries in the bay. It sparkled through the water and created such a bright light that people along the shoreline doused their lanterns.

Another thud hit their raft and two hands, glowing with droplets of algae laden water, pushed their raft towards the shore. The giant grey clawed hands pushed so hard the boys had to hang on, trying to not be capsized off again. The water darkened and fluttered as thousands of fish flapped across the surface. A large, grey mermaid poked her head out of the water, and he saw the similar braids that Himi had worn. Was this her mother?

She winked a big dark eye at them as she gently left them floating towards the dock, flitting under the water to join her pod as they chased the fish back to the bay.

"Here they come!" someone shouted from the shoreline.

The people of Creast ran forward with trinkets and barrels as the mermaids drove the fish forward. The broken surface of the water turned dark as piles and piles of fresh fish leaped from the water and onto the shore. People ran about, catching them with nets, buckets, and their bare hands. Mermaids began throwing the fish from the water, barking with glee as they successfully aimed them into the people's containers. They clicked and called to each other, and several musicians began playing on the shoreline, urging the mermaids on.

Wolflock and Mothy climbed onto the dock and squeezed amongst the people lining the space. A few people fell in, laughing, while their friends reached down to pull them out. After some time of collecting fish, people stored their barrels away for the Winter. The music flowed around them and the people of Creast danced on the harbour wall. Several stayed by the water to touch the mermaids' hands and give them little shell trinkets or human food. The bay was crystal clear.

While the people of Creast collected their bounty,

Wolflock and Mothy watched the mermaids circle. They swirled the water until the moonlight had a completely clear path to all of them, moving the algae towards the edges of the bay. Their rotund grey and black forms all swam in a deosil direction, weaving up and down in the water around the brilliant blue light from the moon and the gemstone. As they weaved, some of them spiralled around each other and join hands, swimming together.

As the evening fell into its celebration, the boys made their way back to the shore. Wolflock was glad they had concocted their raft idea when he saw the mayor, Jaimeron and Girid arriving. If they had waited, they would have missed everything.

As Wolflock and Mothy jogged up to them, Dr Qwan turned away, accosted by a tall woman with wiry red hair.

"Who-"

"That's his wife," Wolflock answered Mothy's question before he could finish it.

"How-"

"They're wearing the same wedding bands and she has a medicine bag on her hip. Also, no one else has confronted him quite so vehemently, and he joked earlier about telling a woman named Charma that Jaxarna was still working, to which she responded she wouldn't want to upset her."

"Oh. And I suppose you never want to upset a fiery spouse."

Dr Qwan was smiling brightly at his wife, who was shaking her hands about.

"Helping? Helping!" she shrieked and her entire face went as red as her hair.

"And now that I'm done here, my dear, nothing shall stop me from wrapping my arms about you and carrying you off to watch the moon rise together," he swooned, both hands clapped to his heart, gushing about his own romanticism.

"If I hear one more word about you helping and not seeing your patients, I'm going to-"

"Excuse me?" Wolflock interjected as he addressed Dr Qwan Loong's wife. "It's a pleasure to meet you, Dr Charma. I-"

"I beg your pardon. Have we met? How do you know me?"

"Dr Qwan has been integral to helping cure all the patients in Creast. If it weren't for his water analysis, we wouldn't have been able to heal the bay and keep the mermaids safe."

"Oh goodness. Such flattery. Best not let anyone hear, otherwise they'll think I'm actually a good doctor.

Charmainette, my darling dear, may we retire to a comfortable back alley so this young apparel intriguer can sing my praises?"

Wolflock's grateful face dropped and Mothy snorted at how similar the faces of the young boy and Dr Charmainette looked.

"Is this why you've missed all of your appointments?" She sighed, gesturing to Wolflock.

"Oh yes! My love, you must hear about Mr Wolflock Felen's infamous plan today. He found out the culprit behind the bay infection, solved who damaged Jaxarna's mine and helped to take out the laziest villain I've ever known."

"And are you going to actually reward him for doing your work for you?"

"Ah! That's my love. As generous as always. Hmm... Let me see..." Dr Qwan dug through his pockets until he found the Antrum bone match. "Aha! It is with my greatest pleasure I can give this token of appreciation to you, Mr clever Wolflock Felen."

Wolflock held his breath as he took the match, struck with delight.

"Oh, don't be foolish. Give him money or a tonic or something-"

"No!" Wolflock said, louder than he intended.

"No, no. Thank you. This is perfect. Thank you."

"Oh? Well, as long as you're happy with it. He's got a bunch of those in the clinic, but if you like it..."

"What a good night," Mothy grinned, hugging Wolflock around the shoulders.

Wolflock said nothing. He just smiled. His friend, Himi, the mermaid who had saved his life, was safe.

"The night's not over yet boys!" Dr Qwan clapped them on the shoulders and got them to stand up. "There is much to be drunk, eaten and danced. Let the best part of the night begin!"

"If you don't see your patients tomorrow, then you'll have demons to pay!" Charmainette warned.

"Of course, my love. Of course! But these gentlemen have never celebrated the Pisces Moon festival! And, even if they had, they haven't celebrated it at Creast! And, even if they had, they haven't celebrated it with *me*!"

CHAPTER 12

A Sleepy Start

Giving no more time for his wife to protest, he ushered them away into the night, where the music played until the dark hours of the morning rose to meet them. They drank tankards of ice-apple cider, ate more food than either thought possible, danced until their feet hurt and their stomachs ached from laughing and singing.

They didn't know what happened towards the end of the night. They were tired, aching, and entirely exhausted from the frivolity of the evening. Wolflock had never had so much fun at a festival before, even though most of that had been by Mothy's lead. They danced with all kinds of people, and finally it whirled into a blur. The next thing Wolflock remembered was waking up for a few moments in a strange room. He could hear Mothy snoring, so he leaned back on whatever piece of furniture he was originally draped over and floated back into sleep with the happy moonlight caressing his face.

* ~ * ~ * ~ * ~ * ~ *

"Loong? Loong, where are you? Your patients are already here!" Charmainette shouted from another room. Wolflock heard her snatch up a pillow and hurl it at her husband. "I didn't book you anyone until midday and you're still late! Useless!"

"Shh.... my dear... I'm hungover..." Dr Qwan rolled over and Wolflock blinked a few times.

The room was a mess. Dr Qwan laid on a single bed in what he assumed was the guest room, and Wolflock had fallen asleep leaning up against the sofa. Books, cushions, blankets, bottles, and stubs of rolled herbal smokes were everywhere. Wolflock vaguely remembered the doctor saying they were too young to smoke, but they could eat all the strange foods they could carry.

Through his bleary vision, he spotted Mothy's

arms and legs coming out at odd angles from the mass of dishevelled bedding, like some strange, jumbled creature. The sun was shining high through the window, stinging his tired, dry eyes.

"Loong, you've missed two appointments already! You said you would be fine to work this morning!"

Two appointments? After a midday start. What a lazy doctor... Wolflock smirked to himself as he curled back up against the sofa. *Midday... two appointments after midday... That didn't sound correct...* His gut twisted and then he sat bolt upright.

"Mothy! Mothy, get up!"

Mothy mumbled and began unwinding his body from the mass of blankets.

"Mothy! We've missed the carriage!"

Dire MYna,

          J kenni ja habe en away osu fumf
meerjungfrau, ja J blid sexder zu hexi ay
netjooxOt ja eany hat J bin niOt par freunde
som ein, aber J bin hat sex erloser. Da left hat
fehlexfreqiO. J exxette alle sex meerjungfrau ein
sex hatfjsen Meer. OffenotliO, trankhexi steuren hir iz
gehexet sen.

          Ja maOe miO frage mehr uns mehr uf jeder
as iz sex hreoen, sex. Groooen sen sex gefleohexeine J
habe muni eany sex hreoen. Oelber hexiexte uns trankheunn
zu hay. Weleohxum ja ja henten hat iz? J hase fumf sex
tag J treff ein hat iz to niOt in sex taO sen leute lifi
sex Thexni.

Dat iz jur en oOnall notexen fumf sex naO fee.

          Wix eany am sex ZoilfuoO Möny Zeoticher
uns sex kline oxeiie iz kemmten zu abelmen oexiexnaO
sexher einetjoder xingeni Zuu sifl eingu sex feotupper
anqany. Dex treoen hix iz heleOex. Da qwexfe habi to. Jo
iz geounde.

          J qwexfe oOxiei afonen oOneel.

Dine exloser bxother,

WolfioO J. Zelen

About the Author

Rhiannon is the walker between worlds. One foot in Earth, the other constantly stepping into Pelaia. As if gazing into a crystal ball, she sees this other world and all that happens within it with the clarity of someone staring through a veil. It is her purpose in life to transcribe these histories, adventures and mysteries for you to enjoy.

This witchy woman was raised by a fairy who taught her that there are all kinds of magic throughout the world. She taught Rhiannon to withhold judgement because you never truly know another's story. She also taught her that everyone, no matter how flawed, has something to give.

The adventures of Rhiannon's youth lead her through trials and dangers that taught her about the darkness within the world, but it also showed her that anything could be overcome. There was always a way. Surrounded by so much apathy and hopelessness, Rhiannon made it her goal in life to show others the light and that if they could dream it they could do it.

The way she was shown this was through stories.

Stories of friendship, love, adventure, discovery, compassion, understanding, and kindness. All of these stories gave her new friends, new lessons, new life.

In the depths of her darkest place during year 11 and 12, when she felt at her loneliest, drugs surrounded her life in terrible ways, the self worth of those she loved and admired crumbled, she was relentlessly bullied and felt friendless in her most trying years, she lived in squalor due to bureaucratic errors, and yet she still had to be "perfect". She had to perfectly excel in school, she had to perfectly remain calm and gentle in the face of abusive men, she had to be a perfect role model for all those around her. That craving for perfection in order to get love nearly killed her several times. In all of this darkness with politicians sacrificing real people and real environments for imaginary money, with teachers displaying no compassion for their students, with men abusing women and children, with communities vilifying those who needed them most, with injustice reigning and all hope seemingly lost... Puinteyle was born.

All of these pains in life were fixed in Puinteyle.

All of them were able to be mended and healed because of a conscientious effort. The people of Puinteyle wanted to be better than their problems. Puinteyle was where people made an effort to love freely and always sought to help each other, animals and the environment. Harmony. True and beautiful harmony. Where the pendulum never swayed too far away from that beautiful harmonious and happy point of balance.

But like in our lives, there is always obstacles to overcome and darkness to understand. Therefore, Puinteyle would always have its own inner turmoils to learn and grow from too. Thus, the stories never truly end.

Rhiannon has always lived and breathed stories, knowing her role in life is to be this guide through a new world for others. Her dream is to support her community with her stories, as well as creating a company where other artists can come together in celebration of Pelaia and all it has to offer.

Become Part of the Magic & Mystery...

www.patreon.com/RhiDElton

If you want more clues, more magic and more mystery, support me on Patreon.

You'll get exclusive clues, maps, sketches, behind the scenes stories, lore and much more! You'll also be the first to know when a new story is coming out so you can solve the mystery before your friends.

If you join at any tier above $10 you can get mugs, posters, bags and shirts, all with your favourite characters.

www.patreon.com/RhiDElton

Thank you for being part of the magic and supporting an independently published Australian author! Australia's independent authors need the support of their local community to continue to produce the books we all love.

If you enjoyed this book, please leave a positive review online (where you purchased the book or on Goodreads), recommend this book to your friends or family, or purchase another copy to gift to a loved one.

Stay tuned for the next mystery in the series:

THE WOLFLOCK CASES

BOOK 8

THE CASE OF THE HAEMATOPHAGOUS EQUINE

www.rhiannoneltonauthor.com

 RhiDElton    RhiannonEltonAuthor

 RhiDElton    rhiannoneltonauthor

 Rhiannon D. Elton   RhiDElton

THE WOLFLOCK CASES